DEAD MAN RUNNING

MICHAEL DYLAN

1

Derrick Morris was scared. Bloody petrified, in fact. He stared at the note in his hand, still not believing it was real, reading the three words on it over and over again, hoping that would change their meaning somehow. But no, there was no mistaking what they said.

HELLO DEAD MAN.

The note was written in blue biro with neat handwriting, all in capitals.

He'd found it in the book he was reading. The book he kept on his bedside table.

The note was bad enough. What was even more terrifying was thinking about who put the note in his book. It should've been impossible.

Derrick Morris was in protective custody, after all, in a safe house in Bethnal Green. Not even his own family knew where he was — not that they cared much about him anymore.

At that very moment, there were two armed police officers sitting in the lounge downstairs, whose very job — their only job — was to make sure no one else got within killing distance of Morris. They'd guarded him for fourteen months, keeping him safe, or so he'd thought, letting no one in to see him except other police officers when they came to question Morris or check on his well-being.

But someone had gotten in. Someone had been in his bedroom and put that note in his book.

HELLO DEAD MAN.

The note that got more terrifying by the second.

It wasn't as if someone could've gotten into the house while everyone was out for a leisurely stroll somewhere. The only exercise and fresh air Morris got was when he did a few circuits of the bloody garden once a day. The rest of the time, he was locked up in the house without even an internet connection to use. So, it was pretty safe to say Morris would've noticed a stranger waltzing into the gaff and going upstairs. But no one had. It had just been him and the police all day and all night long.

That was it.

Therefore, he didn't have to be bloody Sherlock Holmes to work out that it must've been one of his close protection officers who put the note in his book. One of the officers meant to keep him alive was telling him he was a bloody dead man.

It was the only possibility.

One of them must be employed by Elrit Selmani, the gangster Morris was due to testify against in court tomorrow. After all, he was the only man who wanted Morris dead.

Morris closed his eyes. Just thinking of Elrit Selmani made him want to throw up. Memories flashed through his mind of the night his entire world collapsed, the series of bad decisions that were the reason why Morris was holding a threatening note in a safe house in Bethnal Green.

Even now, he wondered why he'd called the prostitute after finding her name card in the pub bogs. He'd practically run over to her place, his hard-on robbing his brains of any sense. He'd all but thrown the fifty quid at her and then he'd jumped on her like a rabid dog. In the end, he was on the bed doing his best not to blow too quickly, and she was on top, doing her best to pretend like she was enjoying it.

Neither of them heard the door open or Selmani come in. In fact, the first thing he knew, he was covered in blood, like someone had tipped a bucket over his head. He'd opened his eyes, seen the girl clutching her throat, trying to stop more blood from pouring out. Then she'd toppled off him and onto the floor.

That was when he first saw Selmani — not that he knew his name then. He was just a scary bloke, grinning like a madman, white teeth shining through his black beard. If that wasn't bad enough, he was holding one of those Rambo knives, all sharp on one side and serrated on the other, with so much blood all over the blade.

It was no surprise, then, that Morris had closed his eyes and screamed and screamed and screamed. He didn't know how long for. But, when he realised too much time had passed and he was still alive, he opened his eyes and found Selmani gone and a dead prostitute on the floor. God knows he should've done a runner then — except he knew there had to be a tonne of his DNA on the girl, in the girl and all over her room. If he'd run, the police would've thought he'd killed it. So, Morris did the right thing and called 999.

It had been the biggest mistake of his life.

Christ, if he could turn back time, he would. He'd never have rung that girl, never gone around to her place, never have gotten himself into this mess.

Morris went to the bedroom window and looked out at the street below. It was Sunday morning quiet, but it'd get busy enough later as people took their kids out or went off to do the shopping. No doubt there'd be a few barbecues going too, as the weather was so bloody nice. If he hadn't called 999 that night, that's what he'd be doing. Enjoying a beer and having a laugh with his wife, Mel, and his daughter, Ashley, while burning a few burgers on the barbie. But no, his family was in France, having told him to fuck off out of their lives, and he was stuck in a shitty terrace house with at least one cop who was going to help someone murder him — or do it themselves.

Shit.

He had to get out of there.

He had to run.

2

Detective Inspector Simon Wise's phone rang, and his heart sank. It was 3 p.m. on a Sunday afternoon and he knew, without looking, that it wasn't someone calling just to say hello. Police officers never get those sorts of calls, even on their day off.

And there was the fact that anyone who might've rung for a casual chat — the few people he considered friends — were all in his garden right then, enjoying the summer sun, laughing away, waiting for Wise to finish cooking some sausages and burgers on the barbecue.

Even his dad was there, sitting in the shade, Stella in one hand, watching his grandkids splash each other in the paddling pool.

With a sense of dread, Wise pulled the phone out of his shorts' pocket and checked the caller ID, hoping that he was wrong, that maybe it was someone trying to sell him double glazing. He'd even be happy if it was a scam artist hoping to trick him into giving away his bank details.

But no. It was Cameron Mace. He was running the protection detail, looking after Wise's star witness in a murder trial. A trial that started tomorrow.

Wise answered the call. 'What's up, Cameron?'

'He's gone, Guv,' Mace replied.

'Who's gone?' Wise said, even though he knew. There was only one 'he' that mattered. The witness.

'Derrick bloody Morris. Bastard smashed the window in the upstairs bathroom and shimmied down the drain.'

Shit. 'How long ago?'

'Half an hour. We went after him soon as we realised what he'd done,' Mace said. 'But he'd bloody vanished.'

'Have you called it in yet?' asked Wise.

'Not yet. I thought I'd better call you first.'

'Well, get on it now. We need everyone looking for him — especially at the train stations and airports.'

'What if word gets to Elrit Selmani that Derrick is out in the world?' Mace said. 'He'll have every idiot with a knife or a gun out looking for him again.'

'You should've thought about that before you let Derrick do a runner,' Wise said. 'We'll have to risk it either way — and who's saying Selmani hasn't already mobilised his troops? Maybe that's why Derrick hoofed it?'

'I'll start making calls,' Mace said, sounding utterly defeated.

Wise knew he should say something to make the man feel better, but he was too angry to bring himself to do that. Mace had screwed up good and proper, so maybe he deserved a bit of time feeling bad about it. Maybe it'd be a learning experience for the man. 'I'll call you when I get into Kennington.'

'I'm sorry, Guv,' Mace said.

'Yeah, you and me both.' Wise ended the call. His wife, Jean, was going to kill him when he told her he'd have to leave the party, but he had no choice. Selmani's trial started at the Old Bailey in the morning but, without Derrick Morris' testimony, the Crown's entire case was going to collapse. The gangster would walk free.

Wise couldn't allow that to happen.

Because Elrit Selmani was about as bad as a human being could get. The Albanian controlled a lot of the drugs, guns and human trafficking business across the capital, and he'd built his empire on the bodies of anyone unlucky enough to be in his way. The Metropolitan Police had been after him for years and, it was fair to say, Selmani wasn't just on the Met's top ten most wanted list — he was right up there at the top.

Eighteen months ago though, Selmani got sloppy and murdered a prostitute right in front of a punter, cutting her throat from ear to ear while she was straddling the poor bloke. For some reason, Selmani didn't kill the witness, Derrick Morris, there and then. Maybe he thought the man would be too scared to say anything or maybe something spooked Selmani because he fled the crime scene, leaving Morris alive.

Surprising everyone, not least the police, Morris called 999 and stayed with the body until the help arrived. The moment he gave a description of the killer, alarms went off in the system and Wise and his team were called in. And, when Morris picked Selmani out of a video identification line up instantly, Wise's team arrested Selmani.

The Albanian had been in Belmarsh Prison ever since, awaiting his trial. Because of all the cutbacks, though, it had taken eighteen months to get a spot in front of a judge and jury.

Eighteen months in which Selmani had tried everything in his power to stop Morris from testifying. The witness came home to find his cat strung up in his hallway with a note stuck to it that said, 'You're next.' He received pictures of his daughter in the school playground with crosshairs drawn over her face and Selmani's men bundled Morris' wife into the back of a van while she was out shopping. They left her locked up in it until a passerby heard her banging and screaming. That was the last straw for Morris' wife. She might've forgiven him for sleeping with prostitutes, but she wouldn't let herself and her daughter be put at risk. She left Morris and went to live in France with her daughter.

Morris, however, still wouldn't withdraw his testimony. Selmani, in response, put a price on Morris' head. It nearly worked too. Someone drove a car into him on a zebra crossing and left Morris with two broken legs and a fractured skull. Then, when he was better and back on his feet, he was attacked in the lavatory in the office where he worked as an accountant. A man stabbed Morris in the back five times. Luckily, for Morris, the company had a member of staff who was first aid trained and she kept him alive until the ambulance arrived.

Since then, the police had held Morris in protective custody. For over a year, Cameron Mace and his team had guarded him night and day, waiting for the blasted trial to start so Morris could point his finger at Selmani and say: 'It was him.'

So, why the hell had Morris done a bunk now? After going through all that? With less than a day to go before the trial was due to start?

Whatever the reason, Wise had to find him fast. He looked around, trying to spot his partner, DS Andy Davidson, so he could tell him the good news. For a moment, Wise couldn't see him, but then he spotted the back of Andy's bald head down towards the back of the garden.

Wise weaved his way through the other guests, ignoring their smiles and hellos, his mind already going over everything that needed to be done if they were to have any hope of finding Derrick Morris.

When he reached Andy, his DS was chatting to Helen, a single mother whose son went to school with Ed, Wise's eight-nearly nine-year-old son. She was good-looking, with curly brown hair, and just the sort of woman Andy enjoyed getting himself into trouble with, despite the fact he was at Wise's house with his own wife and kids in attendance. Maybe it was a good thing Wise was dragging him away. It'd stop Debs, Davidson's wife, from cutting his nuts off with a plastic knife if she saw him flirting with another woman.

'Andy,' Wise said, coming up behind his friend.

The DS jumped at the sound of his name and looked damn relieved to see it was Wise. 'Alright, Si. You gave me a bit of a shock there.' Tall and thin, the man still had a strong Geordie accent, despite Andy living in London for the last twenty-odd years.

'I'm sure.' Wise smiled at Helen. 'Sorry to interrupt, but I need to chat with Andy here.'

'It's no bother,' Helen said. 'I was going to get something to eat, anyway.'

Shit. The food. Wise had forgotten all about it. He glanced back at the barbecue, where he'd left the sausages and burgers cooking and spotted black smoke wafting up into the perfect blue sky. 'You couldn't pop over there and give everything a bit of a turn, could you?'

Helen arched an eyebrow. 'I'm more of a takeaway girl than a chef.'

Wise smiled. 'I'll only be a minute.'

'You better not be more than that,' Helen said, and left them with a wave.

'Jesus,' Andy said, tilting his head as he watched her go. 'No wonder you kept her a secret.'

'Pack it in,' Wise said. 'We've got problems.'

Andy screwed up his face. 'Aw. Do I want to know? I was just enjoying myself.'

'Cameron Mace just called me. Derrick's done a runner.'

That wiped the grin off Andy's face. 'Seriously?'

'He went out the bathroom window and down the drainpipe half an hour ago. Mace went after him, but Derrick was long gone.'

'Shit. The trial starts tomorrow.'

'I know — so we need to find him bloody quickly.'

Andy shook his head. 'I can't believe it. Why now?'

'Something's spooked him, obviously,' Wise said. 'The fucking idiot.'

'Shit. I suppose we've gotta go look for him.'

'Can't see we've got any choice in the matter.'

Andy sighed. 'You told the missus yet?'

'Not yet.' Wise glanced over at the house. His dad had already relieved Helen of her barbecue duties and Jean was standing cross-armed and scowling on the patio, giving Wise that look that told him

Derrick doing a runner wasn't the only problem he had to deal with. 'I thought it was better we tell the wives together.'

'Better for who?' Andy said as they headed towards the house. 'Have I told you Jean scares the crap out of me when she's annoyed?'

'Once or twice — including the night before the wedding.'

'Well, I know you love her and all, but she's not mellowed much over the years.'

Andy wasn't lying there. When Jean got pissed off, she really got pissed off. Still, most of the time she was as happy as can be and a delight to be with. Wise had fallen for her hook, line and sinker the moment they'd met and, over all the years since, he'd not regretted marrying her for even an instant. And, if he was being honest, she was a saint for putting up with him. 'Yeah, well, it's not easy being married to a cop.'

'Especially you,' whispered Andy as they reached the patio. He held out his arms to Jean, despite her stoney-face. 'Way-hey, Jean. How are you, lass?'

'Alright, Andy,' Jean said. The DS wrapped his arms around Jean, trying to hug her, but Jean remained stock-still and gave nothing back.

Andy got the message and let go of her. 'I'm just going to have a word with Debs.'

'You better not be telling me you're going into work,' Jean said when she and Wise were alone.

'I'm sorry, Jean. I have to,' Wise replied. 'There's a drama that needs sorting out.'

'We've got a house full of guests, Simon,' Jean said, unimpressed. 'You promised me you'd be here.'

'I didn't plan this, love. And I wouldn't go if it wasn't important.'

'You're not the only police officer in London. Get them to call someone else.'

'It's not that easy. It's my case. I have the knowledge. We've got a massive trial starting tomorrow, and it's going to collapse if I don't fix it.'

Jean shook her head. 'We've had today planned for months. When was the last time we had everyone around?'

'I'm sorry,' Wise said. 'I really am.'

'Go then.' Jean walked past him and joined their friends in the garden.

'You in trouble?' his dad said, coming over from the barbecue.

'Jean's not happy. I've got to go into work,' Wise said.

His dad eyed him up and down, taking in his shorts and t-shirt. 'Not like that, I hope? I'm not sure the criminal underworld is ready to face the horrors of your white, pasty legs.'

Wise smiled. His father's idea of casual wear was a pair of chinos and a white shirt with the sleeves perfectly rolled up. If he was being honest, it amazed Wise that his dad hadn't turned up at his house wearing a sports jacket earlier. 'No. I'm going to put a suit on.'

'Good lad. You go do what you've got to do,' his dad said. 'I'll cover for you here. There must be a few people here who haven't heard my jokes before and besides, I'm a much better cook than you are. Everyone'll be grateful that they're not eating your charcoal burgers.'

'Great. Jean'll love that.' Wise kissed his dad on the head. 'I'll call you in the week.'

'You do that,' his dad replied.

Wise headed into the house, pausing only to tell Andy he'd meet him by the car out front in a few minutes. The master bedroom was off to the right at the top of the stairs. Walking into it, Wise had a flash of memories, back from when he and Jean had first bought the house. The bedroom had been the first room they'd done up after they moved in, painting it over a long, hot weekend, fuelled by pizza and cold glasses of white wine, laughing non-stop. He remembered the dreams they'd shared, the plans they'd made, and the sex they'd had.

Things had got mundane recently. Half the time, it felt like they were just keeping their heads above water. Everything was getting more and more expensive and both of them were knackered from working all the time — and Wise knew Jean took the brunt of looking after the kids. As delightful as Ed and Claire were, they were a real handful most of the time. Wise felt guilty for not helping more, but The Job took up so much of his time.

Mindful of the time, Wise changed quickly into a dark grey, single-breasted suit, matched with a white shirt and striped tie. He didn't have to put a suit on. He could've just swapped the shorts for a pair of jeans, but Wise enjoyed putting on his 'work clothes.' It got his mind in the right place quickly and allowed him to focus without distractions.

Of course, that was easier said than done when Jean had Ed and Claire waiting for him at the bottom of the stairs, both of them looking heartbroken he was leaving.

'Say goodbye to Daddy,' Jean said with more than a touch of ice. 'He's off to save the world.'

After mouthing 'Sorry' again to his wife, Wise crouched down, so he was eye level with his kids. 'I've just got to go to work for a bit.'

'Are you going to catch bad guys?' Claire asked, seven years old and the light of his life.

'That's the plan, Honey Bear,' Wise said, kissing her nose. 'We've got to keep everyone safe, haven't we?'

Claire smiled. 'I love you, Daddy.'

Ed wasn't so friendly. 'You said you were going to play *Mario Kart* with me.'

Wise ruffled his hair. 'And I will — just not today. You know I'd rather be with you, don't you?'

Ed looked away, cheeks red.

'Hey,' Wise said, pulling his son closer. 'Don't be like that. I really am sorry I can't play with you. I was looking forward to thrashing you at *Mario Kart*.'

That got a bit of a smile. 'You can't beat me.'

'Yeah?'

'Yeah. Even Claire's better than you.'

'I am,' Claire said, giggling. 'You're the worst.'

'Ooh. That hurt,' Wise said, 'even if it might be true. Now, both of you be good for Mummy and I'll see you later.' With one last ruffle of

Claire's hair, Wise stood up and got another glare from Jean, but this one was only half-power.

'Be careful,' she said.

'Bye Daddy,' said Claire.

'See you later, alligator,' said Ed.

'In a while, crocodile.' Wise smiled. 'I love you all.'

Leaving Jean with a kiss on her cheek, Wise headed outside. Andy was waiting for him out in the street by Wise's car. 'You got your bat-suit on, then?'

Wise unlocked his battered old Mondeo. 'I did, but the big question is, did you manage to find your brains?'

They both climbed in. 'I left it back at my house. I wasn't planning on using it on a Sunday,' Andy said.

'Is that why you were chatting up Helen?' Wise turned on the ignition and drove off. Because it was the weekend, cars lined both sides of the street, narrowing the width of the road to a single lane, so Wise had to keep his speed down. His house to Kennington Police Station was about thirty minutes on a good day, but London traffic didn't seem to have those anymore.

'Can you blame me? She's a stunner,' Andy said. 'Even you've got to give her that. And she liked my old Geordie charm, which I always appreciate. So, you know, if she's up for a little bit of the old slap and tickle, who am I to say no?'

'I don't think Debs would appreciate you having another affair.'

'Yeah, well, what she doesn't know won't hurt her.'

'She always knows,' Wise said, turning from Bedford Road into Rupert Road. Then it'd be the Bath Road to the A4 and hopefully a straight run to the nick.

Andy sniggered. 'I can keep a secret, don't you worry. The only time she's ever caught me is when I wanted her to know. You know, you've got to keep the missus on her toes sometimes. It cuts down on the ball busting. You should try it sometime with Jean.'

'Because that'll really solve all my problems.'

'I'm not sure they can get any worse,' Andy said. 'Jean seems permanently pissed off with you.'

'Yeah, well, in my case, it's only The Job that leads me astray. Jean understands that,' Wise said. 'I always make it up to her.'

'Until you don't.'

'You're not exactly making me feel good about leaving her now.'

'Well, when we catch Morris, we can give him a good kicking for ruining our weekends,' Andy said. 'That'll make us both feel better.'

'We've got to catch him first,' Wise said. 'Start ringing around the team. Let's get some more bodies to help us. It'll be better coming from you.'

'Why? Because they like me more than you?'

'Yeah, that's right. I want to ruin your popularity.' Wise turned onto the Bath Road, grateful the traffic was relatively light. That was about the only advantage of working on a Sunday. 'What really bothers me, though, is why did Morris run? It makes no sense.'

'The man's insane,' Andy said. 'If he had any brains, he wouldn't have identified Selmani in the first place, let alone stuck with it after they'd tried killing him for the second time.'

'He's doing it because we promised to keep him safe.'

Andy turned to gaze out his window. 'Yeah, well, that doesn't seem to be working out very well for him.'

Wise glanced at the time. 4:10 p.m. It already felt like they were running out of time to find Morris alive.

3

It took forty-five minutes to reach Kennington Police Station in the end. Andy had wanted Wise to blue light it, but Wise had refused. Being annoyed with London traffic wasn't a good enough reason to put the flashing lights on. All it took these days was one member of the public to complain, and Wise would've been up the creek without a paddle — or more up the creek than he already was.

He and Andy had used the time, though, to think through their next steps and get things moving as much as they could. They'd put a call into DC Sarah Choi and asked her to go over to the Force Control Room in Lambeth. Operated by The Central Communications Command, or MetCal as it was known inside the force, it was where officers monitored London's vast CCTV operations and coordinated communications with police officers on the street. Hopefully, Sarah would find Morris on a camera somewhere and they'd have something to go on.

Andy had also called the rest of Wise's Murder Investigation Team in to hunt down Morris. Those calls had been as well received as could be expected on a Sunday afternoon, but everyone had said they'd turn up and it reminded Wise once again what a great crew he worked with.

Wise had also spoken to his boss, Detective Chief Inspector Anne Roberts, and updated her on the situation. She tossed around words like 'fuck up' and 'a career-ending mistake' just to make Wise feel even better about things. She, too, said she'd come into the station. Wise just hoped he had some progress to tell her by the time she actually showed up.

At least the car park was reasonably empty when they arrived at the station, and Wise got a spot near the front door.

Kennington police station had been around since 1874, but they demolished the original building in 1939 while the fire brigade used the site for emergency water supplies during the blitz. The new station at 49-51 Kennington Road, a rather sad looking building of red brick and utilitarian design, was opened in 1955.

With all the government cutbacks and layoffs, the front desk was closed to the public a few years back and what uniforms remained were sent elsewhere. Now, Kennington was home to some of the Metropolitan Police's Murder Investigation Teams. The MITs investigate cases of murder, manslaughter, and attempted murder as well as other serious crimes. There were twenty-four teams stationed across London, each team comprising fifty officers, which were then broken down into smaller investigating units.

Wise, for the past three years, had headed up one such unit. It was the most fulfilling job he'd ever had within the police but also the worst, as it left little room for anything else in his life. It was no genuine surprise that his problems with Jean started soon after his promotion to the MIT. After all, criminals — especially the worst kind of criminals that Wise had to deal with — didn't work on a nine-to-five Monday-to-Friday schedule.

Wise and Andy buzzed themselves into the nick and headed upstairs to the third floor, to their office, Major Incident Room One or MIR-One. The station itself had an unnatural air to it without all the backroom staff that normally filled it during the week. For some reason, it reminded Wise of the time he and his twin brother broke into their school during the holidays. Every sound seemed to judge them, shouting, 'you shouldn't be here.' It had made it even more exciting back then. Now? Wise wished he was at home with his kids, enjoying a beer or two while eating burnt sausages.

They were halfway up the stairs when Davidson's phone rang. He pulled it out of his pocket and checked the caller ID. 'I'll catch up with you in a minute, Si. I've gotta take this.'

'Alright,' Wise replied, and continued up the stairs to the incident room.

Wise's team comprised ten officers most of the time, depending on what they were working on. Sometimes, other teams pinched officers if they required extra hands or more would be drafted in if Wise had a beast of a case on the go. Budgets being what they were, the one guarantee was he never had more than the bare minimum required to get the job done. Most of the time, his team was juggling three or four active cases, with numerous others waiting to go to trial.

MIR-One was a relic from the fifties. The ceiling panels were stained yellow from the days when every copper smoked at their desks and the grey paint on the walls was chipped and marked. Even the desks bore the scars of serving thousands of officers over the years, with everything from doodles to insults engraved on their surfaces. In fact, the only concessions to modernity were the computers on everyone's desks, but they were a good fifteen years past their best. Even the whiteboards at the other end of the room were far from white. Smears of red and blue and black ink remained where they had put the details of previous cases up and then never quite rubbed out. In some places, you could even make out the ghostly remains of words or names.

The room was empty now, apart from DS Jonathan 'Jono' Gray. With the stomach of a man who loved his food and beer a bit too much, he had his feet up on a desk, twirling a pen between his fingers when Wise walked in. Unlike Wise, he hadn't bothered changing out of his shorts and t-shirt.

'Bloody hell, Jono,' Wise said. 'When was the last time your legs saw some daylight? There are corpses with more colour than you.'

'Me and the sun don't go too well together, Guv,' Jono said. 'I think I was about seven or eight before I even saw it for the first time.'

Wise smiled. 'Well, I hope this is the last time I'm treated to the sight of your chicken's legs.'

'Don't call me in on a Sunday, then,' Jono said. The smile fell from his face. 'That little shit's done a runner, then?'

'Yeah. He has,' Wise replied. 'The question is, why now? He had plenty of time to pull out of testifying and he's spent fourteen months in protective custody, so why wait until the day before the trial starts? All he had to do was turn up at court tomorrow, say his bit, Selmani goes down for life and Morris gets his life back.'

'Something must've spooked him,' Jono said.

'Yeah, that's what I said — but what?'

Andy entered the incident room, a worried look on his face.

'Everything okay?' asked Wise.

'Yeah,' Andy said. 'That was just the wife giving me a bollocking. Apparently, she overheard Helen telling someone she'd given me her number, and she's not happy about it.'

'Ouch,' Wise said.

'Andy, mate,' laughed Jono. 'You're not going to go into hiding as well, are you?'

Andy gave him the finger in reply.

'How long before everyone else gets here?' asked Wise.

'Hicksy, School Boy, Madge, Brains and Donut should be here in the next ten minutes,' Andy said.

Wise nodded. 'Dig up everything we know about Morris while we're waiting. Friends, family, habits, hang outs — the usual stuff. Jono, call Mace and make sure he's got the all-ports warning out. I want every copper at every airport, port and train station on the lookout for him. If ever there was someone who's a flight risk, it's Morris.'

'He won't get far without a passport, will he?' Andy said.

'He's a witness, not a prisoner,' Wise said. 'We wouldn't have confiscated his passport. The question we need answering is whether he had it on him, though?'

'I'll ask Mace,' Jono said.

'Shit,' Andy said. 'Has anyone gone around to his old house? Maybe he'll go there? Pick up his passport and stuff?'

'The wife sold it after she left him,' Wise said. 'He has no home.'

'He must keep his shit somewhere,' Jono said. 'Unless the wife binned it all.'

'Let's find out,' Wise said. 'I'll be in my office. Give me a shout when everyone's here.'

'Alright, Guv,' Andy said.

Wise had a personal office at the back of the incident room. To call it a shoebox would give it credit. There was barely enough room for his desk, a chair, and a filing cabinet. During the summer, it got so hot that he could barely breathe in there and, during the winter, he occasionally had to wear his overcoat to keep warm. But it had a door, and Wise enjoyed his privacy when he could.

Sitting down behind his desk, Wise thought about calling Jean to apologise again, but he dismissed it just as quickly. It was better he left things for now and kept his mind on the job at hand. Anyway, a call wouldn't fix their problems. Maybe he could take some time off after the Selmani trial and go somewhere hot with Jean and the kids. If he was out of the country, work couldn't call him in. He could give Jean and the kids the attention they deserved and they could all have some fun again. Maybe even remember what it was like to laugh with each other. Yeah, a bit of sun, sea, and sand would definitely put things right.

The person he needed to call, though, was the head of Crown Prosecution Service, Jeremy Thurrow, and tell him the good news about Morris.

Wise scrolled through the contacts, found Thurrow's number and hit dial.

'What's happened?' Thurrow said on answering.

Wise smiled. The man was like him. No work call on Sunday was going to be a friendly call. 'Derrick Morris has done a bunk.'

'He's done what?'

'Around 2:30 p.m. this afternoon,' Wise said. 'Smashed a

bathroom window at the safe house and shimmied down a drainpipe.'

'Bugger. Damn. Blast.'

'I used a few more fruitful words, but yeah, it's not good.'

'You're going to find him, though,' Thurrow said. 'You'll get him back.'

'We're searching for him now but there's a good chance Selmani's people are looking for him too.'

'Of course they bloody are. That's why we had him in protective custody.' Thurrow took a breath. 'We're fucked without Morris. We literally have no case.'

'We have the murder weapon with the victim's blood on it, as well as Selmani's prints and DNA.'

'And any good defence solicitor will say he simply found the knife and picked it up without realising what it was. No, we need Morris pointing his finger at Selmani and saying, "It was him."'

'How long have I got to find him?' Wise asked.

There was the sound of shuffling paper. 'I was going to call Morris on day one,' Thurrow said. 'Drop the bomb straight away, but I could move things about so he's our last witness. End our case with the bang. That could work.'

'When would that be?'

'Wednesday.'

'Wednesday?'

'Tuesday would be better.'

'That's no time at all.'

'I told you — we haven't got much of a case without Morris,' Thurrow said.

Wise sighed. 'Can we postpone the start of the trial?'

'How? By saying we've lost our star bloody witness? Selmani's solicitors would just have the entire case dismissed. No, we have to roll the dice and hope we can find him alive and willing to still testify in time.'

'Alright,' Wise said. 'I thought as much.'

'Keep me updated.' Thurrow ended the call.

Wise put his phone down on his desk. Three days. Three bloody days to find Morris alive and not dead in a ditch somewhere.

Shit. Why did Morris run? It made no sense.

There was a knock on Wise's door.

'Yes,' he called out.

The door opened. 'The crew's here, Guv,' Jono said.

Wise stood up. 'Let's get them briefed.'

4

Wise walked back out into the main room to find a bunch of surly faces waiting for him. He didn't blame them. Wise didn't want to be there either, but it was what it was. 'Thanks for coming in, everyone. I'm sorry to ruin your weekend, but time is short.'

There were a few grumbles and grunts in response. Trainee DC Callum 'School Boy' Chabolah cracked open a can of Diet Coke and got everyone looking his way. 'Sorry,' he mouthed. Callum had only been with the team a few months and looked about five years younger than he was. He brought a lot of energy to the team that Wise liked, but the older hands, like Andy and Jono, had come up with the nickname 'School Boy' for him. Wise had tried to discourage it, but it had stuck in the way all unwanted nicknames did.

'The trial of Elrit Selmani starts tomorrow for the murder of Natya Moldovan. Unfortunately, our star witness, Mr Derrick Morris, after a year in protective custody, has decided today is the day to do a runner.' Wise pointed to the picture of Morris that Hicksy had stuck on the whiteboard. The man looked like a beaten-up version of Phil Collins from back in the eighties, all scowls under a widow's peak hairline. 'We have until Wednesday morning to find him, get him cleaned up, in a suit, and ready to take the stand. If we don't, Elrit Selmani will walk free.'

'That can't be right,' said Detective Sergeant Guy 'Hicksy' Hicks. His nose had been broken so many times, it zigzagged down his face like a lightning bolt. 'Selmani's pure evil.'

Wise looked over at Andy. 'Andy, can you take us all through what we all know about Morris?'

Andy walked to the front of the whiteboards and read from the notes in his hand. 'Derrick Reginald Morris. Caucasian. Five foot six in height and weighing in at thirteen stone. Born twelfth September, 1964. Worked in the city for Crown Financial Investments. Was married to wife, Melanie, and has a fifteen-year-old daughter, Ashley. His now ex-wife and daughter have moved to France after Selmani's people made it clear they'd end up dead unless Morris forgot what he saw. Both his parents are deceased, but he has a younger sister, Angela, who lives in Hastings. Records say they haven't spoken to each other in years.

'All pretty ordinary stuff except, on the night of the ninth of January 2021, Morris was feeling naughty. When he saw a postcard in the toilets of the Hare and Hound public house on Masden Street, advertising the services of a prostitute called Tracey with "a good time guaranteed,"' Andy did the bunny ears, air quotes sign, 'young Derrick made a call.'

Hicksy gave a hoot at that. 'Dirty bugger.'

'Tracey was actually a Romanian called Natya Moldovan, brought here illegally by Elrit Selmani. Morris claimed it was his first time using the services of a prostitute, but his wife didn't agree with him on that matter,' continued Andy. 'Either way, Morris went to Moldovan's flat and engaged in sexual relations with her. At some point, Selmani entered the flat using his own key and, for reasons we still don't know, cut the girl's throat while she was on top of Morris, killing her instantly. However, again for reasons we don't know, he left Morris alive.'

'He probably didn't think a perv like Morris would have the balls to ID him,' Jono said.

'Well, apparently Morris did indeed have a massive pair of bollocks because he quite happily pointed the finger at Selmani and the Albanian has been a guest of Her Majesty's in Belmarsh Prison ever since. However, that hasn't stopped Selmani's gang from trying to intimidate Morris into not testifying and, when that didn't work, there were two attempts on Morris' life. That's why, twelve months ago, Morris went into protective custody and there he has remained until today.'

'So why did he do a bunk?' DC Louise 'Madge' Thomas asked. She'd told someone once she used to look like Madonna when she was younger, and they'd called her 'Madge' ever since.

'A good question and one I want the answer to,' Wise said. 'Can you go with Donut to the safe house and have a nose around? Talk to the neighbours, see if they've seen any strangers hanging around. Maybe even discover why Morris ran.'

'Will do, Guv,' Madge said.

'I'm driving,' DC Ian 'Donut' Vollers said from the other side of the room. He was tall and stick thin, almost uncomfortably so. Someone had once commented that he needed a donut to fatten himself up, and a nickname was born.

Madge laughed. 'In your dreams, sweetheart.'

'Callum,' Wise said, ignoring the banter. 'I want you to get onto Morris' bank. If he uses his debit or credit cards, I want to know immediately. Whatever he's planning on doing, he'll need cash.'

'Might be hard on a Sunday,' Callum said.

'Track down whoever the bank manager is and go around to his house if you have to,' Wise said. 'Just get it done.'

'Yes, Guv.'

'Brains,' Wise said.

DC Alan 'Brains' Park looked up. 'Yes, Guv?'

'Talk to the wife in France. Make sure she understands how important it is for her to get in touch with us if Morris contacts her. Find out if there's anyone who Morris might go to for help. Jono, Hicksy — you go down to Hastings. Chat to the sister and make sure you have a look around her house. Who knows — they may not be as estranged as they made out. Could be that Morris thinks a little getaway to the seaside is exactly what he needs.'

'At least Jono's dressed for the beach,' Hicksy said. 'Even if his legs could do with some of the old Ambre Solaire.'

That got a laugh off the troops, but Wise clapped his hands, getting their attention back on him. 'Enough jokes now. It's 5 p.m. now. We have until 9 a.m. on Wednesday to find Morris alive and well. If Selmani's people know Morris is out in the wild, they will hunt him too. We need to find him, ladies and gentlemen, as quickly as we can. I don't want to be investigating his murder and I don't want Selmani back on our good streets. So let's move fast. The clock is ticking.'

5

Andy Davidson sat in a toilet stall in the nick's bogs, wondering just how he'd managed to get himself in so much shit. He knew he'd been on a slippery slope for a while now, but he'd justified things in his mind, telling himself that no one really got hurt by what he was up to — or, if they did, it was because they deserved it.

But this was a whole different ball game.

His heart had sunk when his phone had rung earlier, and the caller ID said it was 'DEBBS WORK.' It wasn't his wife, for one thing. She might want to cut his balls off now and then, but she didn't scare him like the real caller did. He had Davidson's nuts in his grip, and he wasn't letting them go for anything.

He'd waited until Wise was out of sight before answering. 'Yeah?'

'Hello Andy.' The man's voice was pure London, born and bred. 'What are you up to, mate?'

'This and that. Enjoying the sunshine.' Andy forced the words, trying to sound natural, when, really, he was petrified. What did the wanker want?

'Really? So how come you're at Kennington then?'

Andy closed his eyes. Of course, the bastard bloody knew where he was. He glanced out the window, half-expecting to see the caller standing on the pavement opposite, staring up at the station, but he was never that careless. He was a man who stayed in the shadow of shadows. 'There's a drama that needs sorting out.'

'Dear old Derrick has really got a knack for ruining people's lives, hasn't he?'

'Mainly his own.' God, Andy wanted to puke.

'We both know that's not true,' the man said. 'Derrick's going to cause a fair few problems for a friend of mine this week if he turns up at court.'

'Well, he's done a runner now, so your mate needn't worry.'

'There's still time for him to turn up though, and that won't do. Not at all. So, I need to you to fix things a bit more permanently.'

'Look, I gave you the names of his protection officers. I can't do any more than that. Surely Morris doing a bunk is enough? We'll not find him in time for the trial.'

'You can't guarantee that and Elrit is like a brother to me — in fact, I care more about him than I do my actual brother. That's why I don't want Derrick screwing up his life, if you know what I mean. All it'll take is young Derrick turning up somewhere in two weeks' time and we're back to square one.'

'That's not my fucking problem. Elrit should've thought about all this before he cut that hooker's throat,' Andy hissed. 'Anyway, find someone else. I've done my bit.'

The man laughed. 'Oh no, you haven't. Not yet. In fact, you're a long way from being done.'

Andy felt his guts twist a bit more, nausea swirling. 'What do you want me to do?'

'You're going to be a good boy and find him for me,' the man said.

'And what happens if I do that?' Andy asked, but he knew. He damn well knew what was going to happen.

'We'll help Morris disappear properly.'

Andy walked away from the stairs and down an empty corridor. 'I can't do that. I'm a police officer, for God's sake.'

'You're a police officer who likes his drugs and his women a bit too much, Andy. You're a police officer with expensive habits that your police salary can't cover. That's why you're a police officer who works for me doing bad things.' The man chuckled. It wasn't a pleasant sound. 'So, you're going to do this for me, too. When you find him, you call me — or they'll be hell to pay.'

'I'm working with Simon,' Andy said. 'How the hell am I supposed to call you, let alone let you take Morris, if we find him? Si will have him down the nick before I can even get my phone out.'

'That's your problem, not mine,' the man said. 'You deal with that wanker.'

'You're asking too much,' Andy said. 'This isn't what I agreed to.'

There was a pause. 'You remember Sonya?' The man's voice was cold and cruel.

Andy took a breath. Of course, he remembered Sonya. 'What about her?'

'Turns out she's a naughty girl in more ways than you know. Apparently, she filmed you and her last week.'

'She did what?'

'I must admit, I thought I was a broad-minded man, but even I was shocked at what the pair of you got up to. You are quite the kinky devil, aren't you, Detective Sergeant Davidson? And the drugs! I'm amazed you could still get it up with that much Charlie going up your snout.'

Shit. That bitch. 'You bastard.'

'Sticks and stones and all that,' the man said. 'But a video will really hurt you.'

Images of the night with Sonya flashed through his mind — what he could remember of it. He'd been more wasted than he had been in a long while and Sonya had encouraged him to keep doing more the whole time. The coke had been her treat, she'd said and, like an idiot, he'd not questioned it. He'd been too busy shovelling it up his nose to care. And the drugs weren't the worst of it. Not if she'd filmed him.

How could she do it to him? Andy had known she was a whore but, for some stupid reason, he really thought she liked him. She certainly didn't treat him like a punter.

Jesus Christ. How could she bloody film him? Fuck. 'Alright. You can screw me over, but what you're asking ... It's just not possible. There's an entire team of us hunting Morris right now. I don't know how I can give you a heads up so you can get him before we do.'

'You're a smart man. I'm sure you can work something out. Now, I'm going to send you a picture or two just to help motivate you,' the man said. 'Speak to you later.'

The line went dead. A second later, Davidson's phone pinged. A text message from 'DEBBS WORK.' He opened it. It was a picture of Andy, balls deep in Sonya. He barely had time to delete the image before the phone pinged again. Another picture of Andy, naked in front of a tray of cocaine, about to stick a note up his nostril. He deleted that one too.

For all the good it would do.

He could barely remember the briefing after that. God knows what he'd been like when Wise had called him up to do his bit. His bloody hands were shaking, he was sweating, and he thought he was about to puke his guts up.

The moment they were done, he'd legged it to the bogs and shut himself away while he tried to think his way out of the mess he was in. Not that he'd had any bright ideas.

Maybe he could front his way out of it if the video became public. Debs would go mental, of course, but it wasn't as if there was footage of him handing money over to Sonya. He could claim it was just a one-night stand. Blame it on the whiskey and the Guinness. Offer to go to rehab for the drugs. It'd be shit, but not catastrophic.

But it wasn't just the one night he had to worry about.

Anyone with half a brain from Professional Standards would take all of two minutes to work out he couldn't have afforded his house on his salary and that was before anyone looked at the cars and the holidays. Even most of Debs' jewellery had come from less than legal means. Maybe if he was Boris bloody Johnson, he could huff and puff his way out of it, but he wasn't. He was a dumb Geordie who could expect a good stretch inside instead.

Andy had no choice. He had to do what that bastard wanted.

Andy took his wallet out. He'd stashed a small bag of cocaine in it earlier when he thought he was going to be having fun at Wise's barbecue. Well, he wasn't having fun now, but he sure as hell need a pick-me-up.

It took him a moment to get the bag open with his shaking hands. The crack of the seals coming apart seemed ridiculously loud in the bathroom, and Andy froze for a moment, listening for anyone else who could be nearby, even though he knew no one else had entered the toilets. Cursing his own paranoia, he dipped a key into the coke and then transferred it to his nose.

He snorted it, then stuck another bump up the other nostril, snorted that too. God, it stung. Sniffing, he resealed the baggie and slipped it back into his wallet just as someone entered the toilets.

Andy wiped his nose and rubbed his face, making sure there weren't any tell-tale white flecks to give his game away. Still, he didn't move from his little throne, waiting instead for whoever it was to finish peeing and leave him alone.

Waiting wasn't a bad thing, anyway. The coke had his mind and his heart racing, so Andy needed a couple of minutes to get himself sorted and normal out. Then he could go out and fix this mess.

He took deep breaths, trying to stay calm, while the other man finished peeing and washed his hands. Whoever it was took an age doing that too, no doubt singing 'happy birthday,' or whatever crap it was, to make sure they washed their hands long enough to get rid of all the germs. More bloody Covid nonsense.

Finally, the door opened and shut, and Andy was alone again. He stood up, flushed the toilet and left the cubicle. Guilty, haunted eyes stared back at him from the mirror. Some days, Andy didn't even recognise the man he'd become, hating all the little steps he'd so happily taken in the wrong direction to end up a bent copper with a drug addiction. The only time he felt happy now was when he was getting fucked up enough that his brain stopped working and he could forget about all the shit he'd done.

Dear God, if he could fix this mess, Andy promised he was going to change. Clean himself up, stop the screwing around and go back to being the police officer he'd always meant to be. Doing good. Helping others. Catching bad guys. He fucking promised. He just needed to get out of this one last mess.

He left the bogs and went back to MIR-One. Jono and Hicksy had pissed off to see the sister and Madge and Donut were off to the safe house, but Brains and School Boy were still there, jabbering away on their phones while Wise stared at Morris' picture on the whiteboard.

A flash of anger ran through Andy at the sight of his friend, looking all perfect in his nice little suit that somehow stopped Wise from looking like a neanderthal. If the man wasn't so prim and proper, maybe Andy could've talked him into helping out or, at least, get him to look the other way, but he knew Wise would never go for anything that wasn't one hundred percent above board. Not good old Detective Inspector Simon Wise. Mr Fucking Perfect. He was half-tempted to smack the smug bastard in the back of the head. See how he liked that.

Wise turned around and smiled when he saw Andy watching him. 'There you are. I was wondering where you'd got to.'

'I was just having a wee crap,' Andy said. 'I think you gave me a dodgy burger around at your gaff.'

'Wouldn't surprise me,' Wise said.

'Have I missed anything?'

'Unfortunately, not. Sarah called from the Force Control Room. There's nothing of use from the CCTV so far, but she's still looking.'

'Shit.' Andy sucked on his teeth, then stopped the moment he realised he was doing it. He almost regretted snorting the coke. Instead of picking him up, it was making him feel edgy and uncomfortable. He couldn't even look Wise in the eye.

'Guv!' Brains called out. 'I might have something.'

'What is it?' Wise asked as he and Andy headed over to Brains' desk.

'I just got off the phone with Morris' ex-wife, Mel,' Brains said. 'She's not a fan of Derrick's. Not since he confessed to her that he slept with prostitutes at least twice a month for the whole time they were married.'

'I don't think he was doing any actual sleeping with them, Brains lad,' Andy said, trying to act like he would normally, as if he wasn't crapping himself.

Brains went red at the comment. He might be a whizz with computers, but he knew shit all about real life. God only knew if he'd ever been with a woman himself. 'Yes, well, she said that all Morris' belongings are in storage at a place in Southwark. Apparently, all his personal documents are in his unit there.'

'That's something,' Wise said. 'He'll have to go there if he's looking to leave the country.'

'She also mentioned he had a best mate from his school days, a Kevin Sanders,' Brains continued. 'They're still really tight, apparently. Morris would use Sanders for an alibi when he was up to no good. She reckons that if Morris was going to hide anywhere, it would be around at Sanders' place.' He held up a piece of paper with an address written on it. 'Brixton, Rushcroft Road, near the market.'

'Good work,' Wise said. 'Andy and I will go see the friend. You go check out the storage unit. See if Morris has turned up there.'

'Will do, Guv,' Brains said.

'I'll meet you down at the car in two minutes,' Andy said to Wise. 'I just want to check on something.'

Wise nodded. 'You got a hunch?'

'It's probably nothing.'

'See you in the car then.' Wise gave Andy a look that got him all paranoid again and feeling guilty. He turned his back on his friend and headed over to his own desk. Sitting down, he tapped at his computer's keyboard as if he was looking up something. The moment Wise left the incident room, he pulled out his phone and sent Sanders' address via text to 'DEBBS WORK' with the message that said, *we're on our way to see if he's there.*

Maybe that bastard would get to Sanders before them, maybe he wouldn't, but Andy didn't know what else he could do. With a sniff and a rub of his nose, he got up from his desk and headed downstairs to meet Wise, wondering just how much worse the day was going to get.

6

Louise 'Madge' Thomas pulled up outside the safe house on Cyprus Street in Bethnal Green. It was a new build, all red brick and cookie cutter design, the IKEA of houses. The street itself was pretty quiet, but that wasn't surprising. It was late on a Sunday afternoon, after all. There was a flat-roofed pub at the end of the road that was still doing good trade, with half its punters spilled out onto the street, enjoying the weather with ice cold beers, but it would be a waste of time asking if they'd seen Morris hotfooting it past. Judging by the state of the place and the look of the clientele, she doubted anyone there would be police friendly. Maybe there might be someone in one of the neighbouring houses who'd seen something, but on a glorious day like this? Most people would probably have spent the day in their gardens, or maybe they'd gone somewhere nice down on the coast. All the things Madge would rather be doing right then. Then again, she'd rather be chopping her own arm off instead of spending another minute with Donut.

She glanced over at the sad little wanker. She didn't know why the man wound her up so much, but he did. Even the way he breathed got her temper boiling, all huff and puff. Like a pervert about to bang one out.

Why the governor always paired them up together was beyond her. If he hadn't clocked the dirty looks she gave Donut by now, she was starting to seriously doubt his detective abilities. Of course, she hadn't actually told Wise that she thought Donut was a waste of skin, but that was beside the point.

Maybe if Donut used some deodorant now and then, she might tolerate him just a little bit more, but no, the twat probably thought personal hygiene was an insult to his masculinity. It was a miracle she'd not thrown up after being trapped in a car with him for thirty minutes. He smelt rank.

The moment she'd parked, Madge was out of the car and gulping down some fresh air — or as fresh as London air got. Christ, even the pollution smelt sweet after Donut's body odour.

'This the place?' Donut said.

'What do you think?' Madge said. 'That I stopped here because I fancied a bit of sun on my face? Of course, it's the bloody place, Sherlock.' She marched up to the front door without waiting for the idiot and banged on it.

Madge cringed as she heard his heavy breathing coming up behind her and did her best to not imagine how Donut spent his evenings. She failed, of course, because God obviously hated her.

At least the door opened quickly.

'Yeah?' a man said, white, five foot nine or thereabouts, with short red hair.

'You Cameron Mace?' Madge said.

'That's right.' His eyes looked her up and down. 'Wise send you?'

Madge held up her warrant card. 'DC Louise Thomas. The idiot behind me's called Donut.'

Mace chuckled as he stepped aside to let Madge into the house. 'He looks like he could do with eating one.'

Madge rolled her eyes. Another bright spark. The hallway from the door was narrow, barely enough room for one person to walk down it without having to turn their shoulders. The stairs up were straight ahead, living room off to the left, kitchen past that.

She walked into the front room, all kitted out by IKEA in beige blandness. A woman sat in an armchair with a cup of tea on the table next to her. She was black and just a little overweight. 'Hello,' Madge said, making room to let Mace and Donut join them.

The woman got up, and Madge saw the pistol holstered on her hip. 'Sharon Keets.' She held out a hand, but Madge ignored it.

'I don't shake hands no more,' she said. 'Covid and that.'

'I do,' Donut said, jumping in like some overeager Labrador. He gave the woman's hand a good pump, no doubt storing up a mental picture of Keets in that tiny brain of his so he could give himself another good pump later. 'I'm Ian.'

'Roll your tongue in, Donut,' Madge said. 'The woman's had a bad enough day without you ogling her.' She turned to Mace. 'My governor wants to know how you managed to fuck up and let Morris get away.'

'Alright, Charm School, keep your hair on,' Keets said. 'It's not like we helped him climb out the bloody window.'

'Yeah?' Madge said. 'I'd be more impressed if you'd just stopped him from climbing out the window.'

'Alright, ladies, don't get your knickers in a twist,' Mace said, stepping between them both. 'We're all on the same side here.'

'I'm not the one with the problem,' Keets said.

Madge took a breath. 'Sorry. I can be a bit of a bitch sometimes.' She glanced over at Donut. 'Some people bring out the worst in me.'

'Yeah, well, as you said, it's been a shit day,' Keets said.

'So, how did he get away?' asked Madge.

'Sharon was in the kitchen making a cup of tea. Morris and me were watching TV when he said he was off to have a crap,' Mace said. 'Thought nothing of it because why should I? After twelve months of him being as good as gold, no one expected Morris to do a bunk.'

'The next thing we know, we hear smashing glass,' Keets said. 'So, we bundle up the stairs to the bathroom, but he's got the door locked. I thought he'd fallen into the shower or something, so we wasted a bit of time trying to get him to respond.'

'Then I kicked the door in,' Mace said. 'But he was long gone by then.'

'You mind showing us?' Madge asked.

Mace led them up the narrow stairs. The landing was about as narrow as the hallway, with two bedrooms and the bathroom. That was easy to spot because of the broken door, half off its hinges. Madge stepped through the gap, taking care not to catch herself on a shard or a splinter. Morris had done a good job on the window, too.

'He used his bedside lamp to smash the window,' Mace said as a way of an explanation.

Madge peered out the window. The lamp was in pieces on the patio down below. The drainpipe was within arm's reach to the right, but, even so, she wouldn't have liked to climb down that way. Too easy to slip and fall and end up like the lamp. 'Morris must've been pretty desperate to get out this way.' She turned back to face Mace. 'Any idea why he ran?'

Mace crossed his arms, suddenly all defensive. 'None.'

'No visitors to the house? No people hanging around outside?'

'Nope.'

Madge sighed, then headed back on to the landing, past Donut and his stinky armpits, and checked out the bedrooms. 'Which one's Morris's?'

'The one at the front,' Mace said.

Madge entered the room. It had a view of the street outside. A good view, in fact. If someone had been lurking, Morris could've spotted them easily enough. The room itself wasn't much, though. A double bed, bedside table with a supermarket thriller on it, a space where the lamp would've been, a built-in wardrobe, and that was about it.

After putting on latex gloves, Madge looked in the wardrobe. Morris' clothes were still there, and a knackered old pair of trainers was on the floor. 'No computer or iPad?'

'No. We don't allow stuff like that. Too easy to communicate with people without us knowing,' Mace said. 'Too easy to track the IP if you know what you're doing.'

'So, what did Morris do all day?'

'He watched TV, read books and moaned about how shit his luck was.'

'He didn't go out at all? Not even to the shops or for a cheeky pint at the local?'

'No. He stayed inside and out of sight all the time — apart from a wander around the garden now and then.'

'What about his meals?'

'The fridge and freezer are full of ready meals,' Mace said. 'Occasionally, we'd get a pizza or a curry delivered, but Morris stayed upstairs the whole time when the delivery guy came.'

Madge looked around the room again, checked under the bed, then lifted the mattress to look under that. Finally, she opened the drawer in the bedside table. Nothing.

'We've already checked everything,' Mace said. 'There's nothing out of place.'

'And no one spoke to him? Or put a note through the door?'

'We're not completely shit at our jobs,' Mace said.

Madge raised an eyebrow but said nothing. Donut was standing behind Mace, looking gormless. 'You got any bright ideas?'

'Well ... Er ... Not really,' Donut said, proving that he was truly useless.

Madge picked up the book. It was about a muscle-bound man who wandered across America, beating the crap out of people. Netflix had just done a show based on it, according to the cover. 'Go outside and knock on a few doors, then. Ask if anyone's seen anything suspicious.'

'Alright.' And, just like that, Donut trotted down the stairs like a good little doggie.

Mace wrinkled his nose. 'That lad needs a good wash.'

'Oi,' Madge said, waving the book at Mace. 'Maybe you need to sort your own life out before you go casting aspersions. If we don't get Morris back, you'll be lucky getting a job guarding supermarket trollies.'

'You really are a charmer, aren't you?' Mace said, shaking his head.

'I'm not here to make friends.' Madge threw the book onto the side table. A small piece of paper slid out of its pages. She picked it up and turned it over. Written in blue biro in capitals were three words. HELLO DEAD MAN. 'Where the fuck did this come from?'

Mace was open-mouthed. 'I don't know. I've never seen it before.'

Madge gave him a hard look. She always considered herself good at reading people, and he seemed genuinely gobsmacked. 'Now we know why he ran.'

'Yeah, but how did that get in here? Only my people have access to him,' Mace said.

'Then one of your people is bent,' Madge said, placing the note into an evidence bag.

Mace shook his head. 'I've worked with them for years. They can't be.'

'If it's not them, it's you,' Madge said.

'It's not me.'

'Then, unless you're going to blame the bloody tooth fairy, it's one of your team.'

Mace looked towards the stairs. 'It can't be one of them,' he said, but he wasn't sounding so convinced anymore.

'I'm calling my governor,' Madge said, pulling out her phone. She scrolled through her contacts, found Wise's number, and hit dial.

Wise answered on the third ring. 'Madge? What've you got?'

'Found a note, Guv. By his bed,' Madge said. 'It says, "Hello dead man."'

'How did it get there?' asked Wise.

'Mace says no one except for his team has had access to Morris.'

'So one of them gave him the note?'

'Looks like it.'

'Okay. Get them all into Kennington. Let's find who's working for Selmani. And send the note for tests. Maybe we'll get fingerprints or DNA off it.'

'Will do,' Madge said.

'Good work. I'll see you back at the station,' Wise said, and hung up.

Madge looked over at Mace. 'He wants your team down the nick.'

'What an effing mess.' Mace rubbed his face. 'I'll go tell Sharon and then call the others.'

'Don't tell them we have the note,' Madge said. 'Let's keep that a surprise, eh?'

'Yeah. That won't be a problem,' Mace said. 'I still can't bloody believe it myself.'

Madge watched him waddle downstairs. She didn't envy the poor bastard; to lose the person you're supposed to be protecting and to discover one of your team was bent was a lot for one shitty day. Still, better him than her.

Madge checked the time. 6:30 p.m. It was going to be a long night. She only hoped they weren't too late.

7

It was a relatively straight run down to Rushcroft Road. Wise
drove his knackered old Mondeo down Kennington Road, over
the A3, and onto Brixton Road. For once, the traffic gods were
smiling on him and they reached Coldharbour Lane twenty minutes
after setting off.

Andy was quiet next to him, chewing on his fingernails as he
stared out the window.

'You worried about Debs?' Wise asked.

'What?' Andy all but jumped out of his skin.

'You're gnawing on that finger of yours and I just wondered if you
were worried about the bollocking Debs is going to give you later.'

Andy smiled. 'Ah, these days it goes in one ear and out the other.
Anyway, I know she's not really mad at me. She knows it doesn't
mean anything and that I love her.' His eyes drifted back to the
window and the crowds filling the pavements. 'Do you remember
when this area was a no-go zone? Now, it's all yuppies and
millionaires eating tofu and drinking fucking soy milk decaf lattes.'

They passed a pub, The Blue Man. 'I remember trying to break
up a fight in there,' Wise said, 'back when I was in uniform. What
started out as a couple of blokes arguing over a girl ended up in a

mass street brawl that nearly started a riot. We had to get half the Met down to restore order.'

'I miss those days,' Andy said. 'When was the last time we had a good scrap?'

'I thought you were a lover, not a fighter?'

'There's still enough Geordie in me to appreciate knocking some heads together.'

Wise said nothing. He was London born and bred, but he could remember being younger and a whole lot dumber and enjoying nothing more than a good ruck. It didn't matter whether it was at the football or down the pub. He and his brother were a right handful, getting their jollies by hurting people. It'd been great fun right until the moment it all went wrong and things went too far.

Until *that* night.

Wise pushed that thought as deep down as he could. There was no pointing digging up the past. Not that he ever really forgot about that night. It was the last night he and Tom had a laugh together. The last time they'd been friends. Their last night out before ...

'This is your fault. You did this. You bastard!' Tom shouts as the prison guards haul him back, hate in his eyes.

Twenty years later, and it still hurt. God, he missed his brother so much.

Wise drove under a bridge, past the Dogstar pub and what seemed a hundred different gastro cafes, then turned left into Rushcroft Road. It was a quieter street with not so many people out and about, with apartment blocks lining both sides of the street. Some were newish builds while others were a hundred years old or more, their interiors carved up into tiny living spaces with eye-watering prices.

Wise crawled along, looking for a parking spot, cursing everyone who'd come to Brixton to eat out and wander around. There was nothing on Rushcroft Road itself, but he finally got lucky on Electric Lane and he quickly slipped the Mondeo into a space before someone else could nab it.

'Where's Sanders live?' Andy asked as they got out the car.

Wise pointed to an old Georgian building thirty yards back the way they'd come. 'In there. Flat Twelve.'

Kevin Sanders lived opposite a white building with a round tower sticking up like some sort of lost lighthouse at the front of it. 'Chaplin House?' Andy said, reading the plaque. 'As in Charlie?'

'Yeah,' Wise said. 'But he didn't live there. His actual home's around the corner.'

'I thought he was American? What the fuck was he doing around here?'

'Nah. He was British. He and his family lived in Brixton around 1910 or thereabouts for a bit. I think they put a blue plaque up outside the place a few years back.'

Andy sniffed and rubbed his nose. 'Wow. You learn a new thing every day.'

They crossed the street to Sanders' building. Wise tried the front door, but it was locked, so he pressed the buzzer for number twelve.

There was no answer.

'Maybe he's out, having a curry,' Andy said.

Wise pressed more buzzers for other apartments. A couple of seconds later, the front door unlocked, and Wise and Andy stepped inside. Of course, the elevator had an out-of-order sign on it, so they took the stairs. Wonderful. There was nothing like trudging up four flights on a hot August afternoon.

Halfway up, they heard footsteps charging down towards them. Wise and Andy stopped a second before a man came charging down. 'Excuse me,' Wise said as the man barged past them, knocking his shoulder, but he didn't stop or even look back.

'What a wanker,' Andy said.

'World's full of them,' Wise said.

They were both sweating by the time they reached Sanders' flat on the fourth floor, but Wise quickly forgot the heat. He could see Sanders' door from the stairwell. It was wide open.

'Shit,' Wise said. He and Andy sprinted the last few yards to the door and looked in. The living room was a mess. Everything had been upended or tossed onto its side. 'Mr Sanders?' Wise called out. 'It's the police.'

There was no answer. Wise glanced at Andy, who shook his head. This wasn't good.

They entered the flat.

'Mr Sanders?' Andy said. 'Are you here?'

'Check the kitchen,' Wise said. 'I'll look in the bedroom.'

The room barely had space for the double bed in it, and there was a wardrobe wedged into the corner. Like the front room, it was a mess. Someone had thrown clothes everywhere, and the sheets were hanging half off the bed. There was no one there though, as far as Wise could see.

Shit.

Then Wise heard a moan from under the bedsheets on the floor.

Wise hauled them back onto the bed and found a man, bloodied and bruised, curled up beneath them. 'Andy! In here!' Wise called, before bending down to check on the man. 'Mr Sanders?'

The man quivered and whimpered at hearing his name, covering his face with his hands.

'You found him?' Andy said from the doorway.

'Yeah. Call an ambulance,' Wise said. 'Are you okay, Mr Sanders? Can you hear me?'

The man whimpered again.

'I'm a police officer, Mr Sanders. We've called an ambulance for you,' Wise said, speaking slowly. 'Are you okay?'

The man's hands fell away from his face, revealing a broken nose, both eyes already swollen shut and turning black, and busted and bleeding lips. Someone had really done a number on him.

'I'm going to help you onto the bed while we wait for the ambulance,' Wise said. 'Is that okay?'

Sanders groaned, but Wise thought he saw a slight nod of the head. It was awkward trying to get into a position to lift him in the tight space, but Wise managed it somehow. Sanders cried out in pain, but there was nothing Wise could do about that. Once he was settled on the bed, Wise placed a couple of pillows under Sanders' head.

'Th ... thank ... you,' the man croaked.

'Let me get you some water,' Wise said. 'I'll be back in a minute.'

Andy was watching from the doorway. 'That's what you call a beating,' he whispered as Wise moved past him. 'You think Selmani's behind it?'

'Who else?' Wise said. 'We must've interrupted his attacker.'

'The man on the stairs?'

'Yeah. Did you get a look at his face?'

'No. He passed me too quickly,' Andy said.

'Shit. How the hell did they know to come here?' Wise said.

Andy shook his head. 'I don't know, Si.'

Cursing his luck, Wise entered the kitchen. It was the size of many people's toilets, but it was clean and tidy at least, and Wise filled a glass up with water. As he did so, his phone rang. It was Madge. 'What've you got?' he said, full of hope that she had something positive to say.

She didn't. By the end of the conversation, Wise could feel his anger bubbling away inside him even more. There was nothing he hated more than bent coppers, using and abusing their positions of trust for their own personal gain. It was no wonder Morris had done a bunk. He wouldn't have had to be a genius to work out one of the people entrusted with his safety had left him the note.

'Who was that?' Andy asked.

'Madge. She found a note threatening Morris at the safe house. She thinks one of the protection team left it for him.'

'Shit.'

Wise nodded. 'Shit indeed.' He went back into the bedroom and helped Sanders drink some water. 'Just sip it. Help will be with you in a minute.'

'Thank you,' Sanders said.

'Do you know who did this to you?' Wise asked.

'A man ... said he had a package ... for me,' Sanders said. 'When I ... opened the ... door, he ... punched me.'

'Did he say what he wanted?'

'Derrick. He wanted to ... know where Derrick was.'

'Derrick Morris?'

'Yes.' Sanders' head flopped back onto the pillow.

'And do you know where Derrick is?'

The injured man's eyes flared open, full of fear. 'I don't ... know who you ... are.'

Wise held up his warrant card. 'I'm Detective Inspector Simon Wise. I'm looking for Derrick too. His life is in danger from people like the man who attacked you.'

'I ... don't know ... where he ... is,' Sanders gasped. 'I told the man that but ... he kept hitting ... me.'

'It's alright,' Wise said. 'You're safe now.' He looked over his shoulder at Andy. 'They say how long the ambulance will be?'

'No. But with all the cutbacks? It could be ten minutes, it could be ten hours.'

Andy wasn't wrong about that. The newspapers were full of stories about how the NHS was at breaking point; understaffed, overstretched, and criminally under-funded.

In fact, it was pretty much like the police service. How any party could claim to be about law and order when all they did was make it harder and harder for that law and order to be enforced was beyond Wise. Then again, he hated bent politicians as much as he hated bent coppers. They were all scum.

As it was, they had to wait nearly forty minutes before an ambulance turned up. They weren't happy that they had to carry Sanders down four flights of stairs in a stretcher, but, for all their moaning, they had no other option than to do so.

'Do you want me to go with him?' Andy asked. 'Maybe he knows something that he's not told us, or I can get a description of the attacker from him?'

'Alright,' Wise said. 'We've got nothing else to work on right now. I'll go back to the nick and have a chat with Mace's crew. Hopefully, I can find out which one's on Selmani's payroll.'

'I'll call you later.'

'Which hospital are they taking Sanders to?'

'Lambeth.'

Wise nodded. 'I'll call you if I've got some news.'

Once Andy had gone with the ambulance, Wise left Sanders' flat in the care of a couple of uniforms and headed back to Kennington.

On the drive back, his mind raced. How had Selmani's people found out about Sanders? How had they discovered the identity of Morris' protection officers in order to bribe one of them? The information had to come from someone in the Met. Someone who knew the details of everything.

It wasn't a long list of people.

Not even DCI Roberts or Detective Chief Superintendent Walling knew all the ins and outs of the case.

Wise had even kept the information away from most of the people on his own team — and the ones that knew? Christ, he didn't want to contemplate one of them being bent.

In fact, the only people that knew about Sanders were Andy, Brains, and Wise himself. The name hadn't come up in any of Morris' interviews, as far as Wise could remember. So how did Selmani's people find out about him? Had Brains blabbed? God, he hoped not, but who else could it be? It certainly wasn't Andy or Wise himself.

He dialled Callum as he drove.

'Guv?' Callum answered, sounding all perky still. No wonder the others called him School Boy.

'Any luck with the bank?'

'Yeah ... Someone's checking now. They promised to call me back in ten minutes.'

'Good. Good. Can you do me a favour while you're waiting?'

'Sure, Guv. Anything.'

'Can you check to see what social media presence Morris has? Facebook especially. I want to find out if he mentions Kevin Sanders anywhere.'

'Sure,' Callum replied. 'That's the man you just checked out, right?'

'Yeah, Wise said, 'except someone got to him before us and beat the crap out of him.'

'Shit.'

'Yeah, shit indeed. After that, call Morris' ex-wife and see if she told anyone else about Sanders.'

'Wouldn't it be better if Brains did that? He spoke to her earlier.'

'No, I'd like you to do it — and keep it to yourself for now. I'll be back at Kennington in ten minutes or so.'

'I'll have it all ready for you then,' Callum said.

'Good lad.' Wise ended the call. He thought about calling Andy and telling him about Brains, but left it for now. It was going to be difficult enough finding Morris without everyone worrying about someone on their team working for Selmani as well.

8

Hastings on a sunny Sunday was no place to be. The traffic was bumper to bumper, and the crowds were everywhere. Jono threw his cigarette butt out the car window in disgust. 'Bloody global warming,' he muttered. 'Summers are supposed to be wet and miserable in this country — not hotter than the Algarve.'

Hicksy laughed. 'I think it's lovely.'

'What's lovely about sweating your balls off? Or seeing fat people showing off skin that no one in their right mind deserves to see?' Jono pointed to a couple waddling along the seafront, lapping at ice creams. The man was shirtless. An array of shit tattoos covered his chest, which only emphasised the size of his belly. The woman was a bit more conservatively dressed, but not by much. 'Look at those two for a start. We should arrest them for GBH looking like that.'

'You know you're no oil painting yourself?' Hicksy said.

'Next to you, I look like David bloody Beckham.'

'In your dreams, sunshine.'

'Nightmares more like.' Jono pulled another cigarette out of the packet and stuck it in his mouth.

'You know it's against the rules to smoke in a police vehicle, don't you?' Hicksy said. 'You could give me second-hand cancer.'

'You know I don't give a toss?' Jono sparked up his lighter and sucked hard on his fag as he lit it. He chuckled as he blew out a lungful of beautiful blue smoke. 'And when did you get all woke?'

'You bastard,' Hicksy said, waving it away from his face. 'You're killing me.'

'How?' Jono said in mock innocence. 'I've got the window open, haven't I?'

'Wanker.' Hicksy turned off the London Road by a Lidl supermarket onto Church Road. He craned forward in his seat as he looked at the house numbers. 'Which one's the sister's?'

Jono pointed to Hicksy's phone stuck to the dashboard. 'Well, Sherlock, according to the satnav, it's fifty yards ahead on the left.'

'Smart arse,' Hicksy muttered just as the phone announced, 'You have arrived at your destination.'

Georgian houses, most of which were broken up in blocks of flats and painted in a host of colours, from white to pink to blue, lined either side of the street. Kevin Sanders' sister's place was lilac. 'Who wants a lilac house?' Jono said, taking another drag.

'Stop moaning,' Hicksy said. 'Just keep your eyes open for a parking spot.'

Jono wasn't looking for parking spots, though. He had his eyes on something — someone — far more interesting. A bloke was walking up the street, munching on a bag of chips. Late fifties, five foot six-ish, bit overweight, little tuff of hair at the front all pulled up like he was doing his best to pretend he wasn't losing it. In fact, he looked exactly like—

Jono threw his cigarette out the window. 'Stop the car! That's Morris.'

Hicksy slammed on the brakes. 'Where?'

Jono was already out the door and sprinting towards the man. 'You! Don't move!'

The man looked up, all wide-eyed and petrified. For a brief, glorious moment, Jono thought he was going to actually do as he was told, but when did that ever happen? Instead, the bloke threw his chips up in the air, turned and legged it.

There was nothing Jono hated more than a bloody foot race. Ten yards on and his lungs were burning and churning up all the muck that came from smoking too much. Twenty yards and he thought he was going to choke. He cursed every cigarette he'd ever had, but still he ran on. His target, though, was opening up a gap on him. If the oik made it to the seafront, he could disappear into the crowds and never be seen again.

Jono tried to find some extra speed in his legs, but the bastard things refused to cooperate. Shit, he was going to lose Morris.

Then Hicksy came pounding past him, moving so fast Jono might as well have been standing still. His partner was on Morris an instant later and hauled the man to the ground, falling on top of him in the process.

Jono stopped running and wheezed, trying to get air into his lungs as if his life depended on it — which it did. Then his gut lurched, a load of bile came rushing up his throat and he vomited all over the pavement.

By the time he looked up and wiped his mouth, Hicksy had Morris in handcuffs and several bystanders were filming the whole thing on their phones. 'Haven't you got anything better to do?' Jono said, waving them off.

'No,' a kid in a giant hoodie said, seemingly impervious to the summer heat.

'Well, fuck off then,' Jono said as he staggered towards Hicksy and Morris.

'You fuck off, Linford Christie,' the kid replied, sticking his finger up in the air.

Jono ignored him. They had Morris. That was all that mattered. He and Hicksy had saved the day. 'You thought you could get away from us?' he said, as Hicksy hauled the man to his feet.

The man looked from Hicksy to Jono and back again and then blabbered something in a foreign language.

'What did he say?' Hicksy said.

'Stop pissing about, Morris,' Jono said, his mouth still stinging from the bile.

Again, the man rattled off more gibberish, looking utterly petrified.

'I don't think he's pretending,' Hicksy said.

Jono stared at the man, suddenly not quite so convinced they'd nabbed the right person. He had a darker complexion and more hair than Jono remembered Morris having. He didn't look like he was in his fifties either. Maybe not even in his forties. Jono sighed. 'Has he got any ID on him?'

Hicksy patted the man's pockets and found a wallet. He opened it up and produced a Euro driving licence. 'Says he's Juan Pascal, from Madrid.'

The man perked up, hearing his name, and spouted off more words Jono didn't understand.

'Bollocks,' Jono said. Looking at him now and at his ID, the man wasn't even that close a match for Morris. All that running for bloody nothing. 'Shit. He's not our man.'

Hicksy unlocked the handcuffs. 'Sorry, mate.'

Pascal snatched his wallet off Hicksy, rabbiting away in Spanish, getting all irate now he wasn't in cuffs.

'Alright, Pablo,' Jono said. 'It was an honest mistake. No harm done.' He tried a big smile, but that seemed to just piss the Spaniard off even more.

A car honked from back up the road. Hicksy had abandoned their vehicle, blocking the street off, to join Jono in his mad pursuit. 'I'd better go move it.' Hicksy patted Pascal on the shoulder. 'Sorry about your chips.'

Jono was damn glad it was Hicksy who had to move the car. He didn't think he had the energy to go two yards right then. One of these days, he'd have to get in shape again. Maybe give up the fags.

Next to him, the foreign geezer was still giving him dirty looks. Jono didn't know the Spanish for 'sorry,' so he just said it once more in English. It didn't calm the man down, but what was done was done, so Jono headed back up to Angela Sanders' house, leaving ole Pascal to rant and rave behind him.

He winced as he passed his little pile of vomit on the pavement and wished he had some water to wash his mouth out. He reached for his cigarettes instead, then cursed when he realised they were in the car still. Jono looked around, trying to spot where Hicksy was parking the motor, but had no joy. All he could do was wait outside the stupid lilac house, his mouth reeking, sweat running down his back, longing for a fag.

It summed up his day, really. Still, it was better than watching the Eastenders omnibus with the missus.

To make things even worse, Hicksy didn't bring Jono's fags with him when he finally turned up ten minutes later, all out of breath himself. 'I had to park in a public car park on the seafront — twenty quid for a couple of hours.'

'Bloody robbery,' Jono said. 'Good luck getting that back on expenses.'

'Surely the bloody pencil pushers couldn't object to that?' Hicksy said, but they both knew they damn well could.

The pair of them trudged up the steps to Angela Morris' front door. There was a plaque next to the doorbell. It said 'Sunshine Rooms' with five gold stars underneath. There was no mention, of course, about who gave the place the rating. Probably Angela herself.

Hicksy rang the doorbell.

A woman answered, and this time there was no doubting the resemblance to Morris. In fact, if it had been Derrick himself, dressed up in drag, Jono wouldn't have been surprised.

'Hello, my lovelies,' she said before either officer could speak. 'You're a little bit early but come in anyway.' She stepped back and waved them into the hallway.

Exchanging a quick glance with each other, Jono and Hicksy entered the house.

'The waiting room's straight ahead on the left,' Angela said. 'The girls you booked are just finishing up with some other customers right now, but you shouldn't have to wait too long.'

'I think you might have us mistaken for someone else.' Jono held up his warrant card once they were in the waiting room — which was just a converted front room with a couple of worn-out sofas and a few mismatched dining room chairs placed along the walls. There was seating for at least twenty people, which made Jono wonder about how many punters Angela could move through the house at any one time and how many girls she had working. Still, it wasn't important right then. 'I'm Detective Sergeant Jonathan Gray and this is Detective Sergeant Roy Hicks. We're from the Metropolitan Police.'

Hicksy held up his warrant card, making no attempt to hide his grin as the woman did a double take.

'You don't look like coppers,' Angela said. 'How do I know those cards are real?'

'Oh, they are,' Hicksy said. 'Don't let his pasty legs fool you.'

'But you're London police,' the woman said. 'This isn't your patch.'

'I'm not sure that's going to help your defence, luv,' Hicksy said.

'Bastards,' Angela said with a shake of her head.

'First, can you confirm you are Angela Morris?' Jono asked.

'I ... Er ... Well ... Er ...' The woman had gone deathly white and was as stiff as a board.

'Are you Angela Morris?' Jono repeated.

'I ... am. Yes.' She glanced over towards the stairs. Probably worried a punter was about to come strolling down with another five-star rating for the Sunshine Rooms.

'We're not interested in whatever you've got going on here,' Hicksy said. 'We're looking for your brother.'

Angela seemed to deflate with that bit of information. 'What's he gone and done now?' She plopped herself down on one of the sofas. She didn't suggest Jono or Hicksy sit down, but they both did anyway and Jono was damn grateful for it too. That bit of sprinting outside had really knackered him out.

'You've not heard from him then?' Hicksy asked.

'I thought he was with your lot,' Angela said. 'For his own safety and that.'

'He was,' Jono said, 'right until he did a runner this morning.'

Angela laughed. 'The man was always an idiot.'

'He's not called you or come knocking at your door?' Jono asked.

'Look — Derrick and me are brother and sister, but that don't make us best friends or nothing. To be honest, he can be a right pain in the arse when he wants to,' Angela said.

'How do you mean?' Hicksy said.

'Growing up wasn't easy for either of us. Our mum, well, she was on the game, so things were always weird at our house. Men coming and going at all hours. Me and Derrick had to look after ourselves a lot of the time and that sort of environment affects you, if you know what I mean.'

'In what way?'

'Mum had friends who were on the game too and, sometimes, they'd work from our house as it was safer and cleaner and Mum only took a bit of their wages for cleaning and stuff. And that was all good and proper, right? Except when Derrick hit puberty and suddenly, he's surrounded by women who'll have sex with him for his pocket money.'

'Derrick was a bit randy then?' Jono asked, trying not to imagine what he would've been like in that situation when he was a teenager. He certainly wouldn't have been wasting his pocket money on copies of *2000 AD* if he'd had the option of something more fun.

'A bit? He was like a dog in heat, humping everything he could,' Angela said. 'Then he had the bright idea of pimping the girls out to his mates at school. They got to lose their virginity and Derrick took a commission that paid for his own shags.'

'What did your mum think of that?' Hicksy asked.

'Well, she was as happy as Larry. Sorting out randy schoolboys was better than dealing with fat, middle-aged men with STDs, if you know what I mean.' Angela chuckled. 'Of course, it was awkward at school when half your mates have shagged your mum.'

'He pimped his own mum out to his mates?' Jono couldn't believe it. He's heard some pretty screwed up stuff in his life, but that was up there.

Angela shrugged. 'Work's work. Money's money.'

'What about you?' Hicksy asked. 'He ever pimp you out?'

'He tried. I told him to fuck off.'

'But you're on the game now?'

'No, I'm bloody not and never have been neither. I facilitate introductions, make sure everything's all hunky-dory and clean up after the mucky sods, but that's it.'

'What about Derrick? He still involved in the family business?' Jono asked.

'Nah. He discovered the city. Said there was better money in fucking people over than there was in fucking them. He still liked it, though — sleeping with prostitutes. He used to come down here on the pretence of seeing me, just so he could spend the weekend up to his nuts with the girls.' Angela shook her head. 'Except the dirty bugger never wanted to pay — so we had a falling out and I told him to bugger off. That was a good three years or so ago and I've not heard diddly squat from him since then.'

Jono sat forward. 'But you knew he was in protective custody?'

'Word gets around,' Angela said. 'It seems like at least half the girls these days work for Selmani or did at one point. So, him getting banged up was big news.'

'But he didn't call you or you call him?' Hicksy asked.

'Funnily enough, no,' Angela said, her voice dripping with sarcasm. 'I didn't think it was that smart to advertise the fact that Derrick is my brother. I don't want no trouble knocking on my door.'

'So he's not here?' Jono said.

'No, he's not.' Angela sat back and crossed her arms. 'He knows he's not welcome.'

'You won't mind us having a look around, then?' Hicksy said.

'You've got to be joking, ain't you?' Angela said, scowling. 'I can't have coppers sticking their noses in the bedrooms. People expect a bit of confidentiality when they're going about their business here.'

'You either let us do it,' Hicksy said, smiling, 'or we make a call to the local plod and get them to do it. If that happens, we'll probably have to bring you, your girls, and your punters down to the station for questioning. I'm sure that'll do wonders for your business.'

'Wanker,' Angela said.

'Only occasionally,' Hicksy said. He stood up. 'Shall we do this the easy way, then?'

'Can you at least wait until the two blokes upstairs are done?' Angela asked. 'They'll probably won't be more than another ten minutes.'

'Depends if you're going to make us a nice cup of tea while we wait,' Jono said. 'I'm parched.'

Angela stared daggers at him, but Jono was immune to that shit. Being married for twenty odd years had made him a master at ignoring a woman's hard looks. He smiled as Angela got to her feet and headed towards the kitchen. 'And if you've got a spare cigarette hidden away back there, I'll have one of them too,' he called out after her.

'You really can be an annoying twat sometimes,' Hicksy said.

Jono gave him a wink. 'Call the boss, eh, and tell him it's a bust down here.'

9

Wise sat in Detective Chief Inspector Anne Roberts' office, telling her the good news. She was about ten years older than Wise, with short, silver hair that accentuated the lines hard set on her face. She had no lips to speak of either, which made her mouth appear to be just another one of those lines. Roberts was a good boss, though — most of the time. Smart and always to the point. She could be brutal with it occasionally. Especially when she wasn't happy, like she was right then. Getting dragged in on a Sunday to work would piss off most people, but hearing you might have a dodgy copper on the team was the icing on the cake.

'You can't be bloody serious,' she said. 'This is a disaster.'

'According to Madge, the only way they have could've passed the note to Morris was via one of the protection officers. And the only way Selmani's gang could've learned their identities is from someone on my team,' Wise said.

'And you reckon its Brains?'

'The only people that knew about Morris' mate and where he lived were me, Andy, and Brains. There's no way Selmani's people just found out about Sanders at the same time as us. Someone must've called them and passed the information on.'

'Where's Brains now?' Roberts asked.

'He's checking out some storage lockers where Morris' ex dumped his stuff,' Wise said.

'Do you think that's smart? Shouldn't you call him back here and question him?'

'I've got no proof at the moment,' Wise said. 'And I'm not tarring his reputation just on my suspicions.'

'Alright,' Roberts said. 'It's your call.'

Great. In police-speak, that meant: 'I don't agree with you, so if it goes tits up, you're to blame.'

Wise nodded all the same. 'We're bringing in Mace's team now to find out which one of them is bent, too.'

'I don't need to tell you what a fuck-up this is, Simon. If Morris turns up dead and Selmani walks, there's going to be a shitstorm coming our way, especially if it turns out coppers from this station helped make it happen.'

'We're doing the best we can. I'm confident we'll get Morris back alive.'

'Good. Keep me updated,' Roberts said.

Wise left Roberts' office and headed back to MIR-One, wondering why he hadn't hauled Brains back to the nick. He should do. Leaving him out in the wild, chasing leads, wasn't a smart move if Brains was on Selmani's payroll.

Wise just couldn't shake the feeling that he was wrong about Brains, though. After all, whoever was on the take knew who the protection detail was and, as far as Wise knew, Brains didn't have a clue who they were — unless he'd hacked it off a computer system somewhere.

Callum was waiting for Wise on the stairs. 'Guv, I've got that information you asked for.'

'Tell me,' Wise said.

'Morris deleted all his social media accounts soon after the incident with Selmani, on our advice,' Callum said. 'So there's nothing there about Kevin Sanders.'

'Right,' Wise said. 'What about the ex?'

'I spoke to Mel Morris and the only person she'd mentioned him to was Brains.'

Neither of those were answers Wise was hoping for. He wanted other suspects to blame for what happened, but now Brains was even more in the frame. 'Good work, Callum. Appreciate it.'

'No problem, Guv. Anything else you'd like me to do?'

'No word from the bank yet?'

'They said there's been no use of either his debit card or his credit card, but both cards are still active.'

'Can you meet up with Brains at the storage centre? Help him keep an eye out?'

'Sure thing.'

Wise patted him on the shoulder. 'Good lad. Keep me informed if anything crops up.'

'Will do, Guv.' Callum ran off as eager as a puppy, leaving Wise to continue on to MIR-One. He was almost there when his phone rang. It was Madge.

'What's up?' he asked on answering.

'I need you to come over to Hackney, Guv,' Madge said.

Wise didn't like the sound of her voice. 'Why?'

'Mace rang around his team to tell them to come to the nick,' Madge said. 'Except one of them, Tarik Gardner, didn't answer. Mace said he lived close to the safe house in Hackney, so we drove over to pick him up.'

Wise closed his eyes. 'And?'

'He's fucking dead, Guv. Throat cut from ear to ear.'

The same way Selmani killed the prostitute. Shit. 'Have you called for forensics and the pathologist yet?'

'Yeah. They're on their way,' Madge said.

'Alright. Give me the address and I'll come straight over.'

'It's the blocks of flats on Brenthouse Road. Seventh floor.'

This time, Wise did blue light it across London to Hackney, and he was there twenty minutes after hanging up the phone with Madge, arriving at the same time as the forensics team. The block of flats was a red brick building with rows upon rows of white windows that made it look like the world's most boring game of *Tetris*. It didn't look a great place to live, let alone die in.

Wise knew he should wait for the Scene Of Crime Officers — SOCOs — to get set up and do their initial search before he looked at the crime scene, but that could take hours and the clock was ticking. He ran into the building and took a piss-stinking, graffiti-scrawled lift to the seventh floor.

Madge and Mace were waiting in the hallway, both white-faced and as grim-looking as a person could get. The door to Gardner's flat was open.

'Forensics are downstairs,' Wise said, 'but I want a quick look first.' He pulled on some blue latex gloves.

'He's this way,' Madge said, and pushed the door open. She led him down a narrow hallway made narrower by a bunch of coats hanging on hooks by the door, past a toilet and into the living room.

There wasn't any need to go further. Gardner was sitting in an armchair, facing the TV. A red gash ran from one ear, under his chin, to the other ear, and blood had soaked the front of his shirt and trousers bright red. The killer had shoved a bunch of twenty-pound notes in his mouth.

'I don't think he's been dead that long,' Madge said. 'When we got here, the blood on his shirt still looked wet.'

'I'd guess he's our inside man,' Wise said, 'and they've killed him to stop him talking.'

'Yeah,' Madge said, 'but they're not exactly hiding who's behind this.'

Wise nodded. 'Let's get out of here. Hopefully, the SOCOs can find us something so we can nab whoever did this. Our priority, for now, still has to be finding Morris.'

They left the flat just as the SOCOs were coming out of the lift.

Madge pointed to the open door. 'He's in there.'

Wise got out of their way. 'I'm sorry about your man,' he said to Mace.

'Stupid arse,' Mace said with a shake of his head. 'He was the last person I'd have thought would get mixed up with gangsters.'

'Maybe they had something on him,' Wise replied.

'Well, he should've come to me. I could've helped him.'

'You suspected nothing?'

'Of course not. You never do, do you? Not when it's your team.'

Wise thought of Brains. He still didn't believe he was bent, even though the facts said otherwise. 'I'm sorry again,' Wise said to Mace, then he turned to Madge. 'I'm going to go down and make a call, then head back to the nick.'

'I'll catch up with you there,' she said.

Wise took the lift back down to the ground floor, holding his breath in a vain attempt not to breathe in the stink.

Once he was outside, he took out his phone and dialled Andy.

'Alright, Si,' Andy said. There was traffic noise in the background.

'Where are you? You not at the hospital?'

'Aye, I am. But I've just stepped out to get some air. I hate these places. They're full of sick people.' He sniffed. 'How's it going? Any joy in finding the git?'

'Madge found a note threatening Morris at the safe house. One of the protection officers had given it to him.'

'Bastard. Any idea who?'

Wise sighed. 'Yeah. A bloke called Tarik Gardner.'

'You nick him already?'

'No. Someone cut his throat open before we could get to him, then stuffed his mouth with a load of cash.'

There was a pause. 'Fuck.'

'These people aren't messing about,' Wise said. 'God knows how they're getting the jump on us all the time. I think ... I think they've got someone on our team helping them.'

'You think what?' Andy's voice was shocked.

'It's the only thing that makes sense,' Wise said. 'I think it might be Brains.'

'Brains?'

'Yeah. He knew about Sanders. He knew about the safe house.'

'So did you and me,' Andy said.

'Yeah, but I know you and me didn't do it. That only leaves Brains,' Wise said. 'I can't believe it, but it's the only thing that makes sense.'

'What are you going to do?'

'Callum's with him for now. I need more proof before I drag him in, though. I can't ruin the man's career just going on my gut.'

'Brains is a good lad, Si.'

'I hope you're right,' Wise said. 'How are you getting on? Any luck?'

'I've got nothing. The doctors gave Sanders something for the pain and he's been out cold since. They reckon it'll be a while before he wakes up again.'

'You okay to stay with him?'

'It's nae bother.'

'Will Debs be okay with you working late?'

Andy laughed. 'She's got no choice in the matter. She knows what side her bread's buttered on. More importantly, what about you and Jean? She was pissed with you, man.'

Wise winced. 'I should call her.'

'You should.'

'Don't really need another bollocking, though.'

'Who does?'

'Let me know if you get anything from Sanders, eh?'

Andy sniffed again. 'Aye, will do.'

'And look after yourself,' Wise said. 'Sounds like you're getting a bit of a cold.'

There was a pause for a moment as Wise listened to cars drive past. 'Speak to you later,' Andy said and ended the call.

10

Lambeth Hospital was a miserable place. It was due to be closed within the next year and, as such, the council had starved it of love and funds for a damn long time, leaving the place looking like it was on its deathbed. Paint was peeling off the walls, and half the wards were out of use. The parts that were still staffed only had skeleton crews looking after the patients.

Even the hot drinks machine was a collector's item from the seventies, spitting out sludge into plastic cups so thin, they were impossible to hold without burning your fingers.

Not that Andy was thinking about a cup of tea right then. He was in a battered toilet cubicle that was covered in graffiti, chopping out another line of coke on the top of a toilet cistern that dated back to the fifties. He knew it wasn't a good idea, but he needed the buzz to keep going and to stop himself from thinking about the shit he was in.

The call with Wise had sent him reeling. He couldn't believe they'd cut Gardner's throat and yet it was exactly what that bastard would do. A handy reminder of what Andy could expect if he let him down, too. It didn't help that Gardner's death was down to Andy, either. He'd given the names of the protection group to the bastard, knowing full well they were going to put the screws on someone to get access to Morris.

Andy had justified it by convincing him the bastard would just put the scares on Morris, that no one would get hurt by what he'd done. Another lie and not a good one. Then again, Andy was an expert at believing his own bullshit.

Still, none of that helped with his present predicament. He needed to find out where Morris was before the bastard cut Andy's throat or, even worse, his family's.

The hospital had put Sanders in a private room. Unfortunately, though, they'd given him something for the pain that had knocked him out for the duration, which made it impossible for Andy to question him. Instead, he'd been sitting like an idiot by the bloke's bedside for the past few hours, waiting for Sanders' drugs to wear off while topping up his own.

Speaking of which, Andy stuck a rolled up five pound note up his nostril and hoovered the cocaine off the top of the cistern. It burned as he inhaled and he had to gulp as it dripped down the back of his throat, but he felt his tiredness lift and his senses spark up.

He could do this. He could get himself out of the shit he was in. Sort it out, then get out. No more dodgy stuff. No more working for the bastard. He'd been a good cop once and he could be a good cop again. Even be a good husband again. Knock the drugs on the head. Stop screwing around. Maybe even give up the drink.

Maybe. Maybe. Maybe.

Stuff to think about another day. Another night. Tonight, he had things to do. A fucking twat to find.

He pulled the chain of the ancient toilet, slipped the note in his pocket, rubbed his nose just in case, then left the cubicle. The florescent lights of the toilet made him blink, then the sight of himself in the mirror made him wince. For a moment, he thought about getting the bin and smashing the mirror to bits, but he needed no more bad luck.

He marched back out into the corridor and down to Sanders'

room. The prat was still asleep. Closing the door behind him, Andy went up to the bed.

The hospital had patched Sanders up, wiped the blood off, reset his nose, and put plasters over the cuts that didn't need stitching. His right forearm was broken, but that wasn't due to be set until the following morning, according to the nurses. The bloke had three broken ribs as well to go along with all that damage. Whatever scrote Selmani had sent along to sort Sanders out had done a damn good job on him.

Still, Andy didn't have all night to wait for Sanders to wake up. He needed answers, and he needed them right away.

He went back to the door and checked that there was no one about. Satisfied that he was alone, he shut the door and returned to Sanders' side.

'Sorry, mate,' he whispered, then squeezed Sanders' right arm where the break was. It didn't take long for Sanders' eyes to pop open. Andy clamped his other hand over the twat's mouth so he couldn't scream out, then squeezed some more. Sanders flapped about a bit, trying to get free, but he wasn't going to go anywhere banged up like he was.

Andy leaned in so Sanders could see him. 'Hello.'

Sanders tried saying something back, but it was all muffled gibberish with Andy's hand over his mouth.

'Now, I know the man who beat you up got interrupted before you could tell him anything, so I'm going to ask you some questions instead,' Andy said. 'You tell me what I want to know, and I'll leave you alone. Scream for help or lie to me and I'll make the kicking you've already had feel like the best time of your life. Now, nod your head if you understand me?'

Sanders nodded.

Andy removed his hand. 'Now, where is your good friend, Derrick?'

'I don't know,' Sanders grunted.

Andy covered his mouth once more and gave Sanders' broken arm a good shake. The man gave out a muffled scream, eyes bulging, body thrashing. After a minute, Andy released the arm but kept the man's mouth covered until he'd quietened. 'Where's Derrick?'

Sanders' breath came out in panicked snorts out of his nostrils until Andy let go once more of the man's mouth. 'Who are you?'

'That's not important, Kevin lad. You answering my questions is — now, where's Derrick?'

'I swear to you, I don't know. I haven't seen him in over a year.'

Andy leaned in until their noses were almost touching. 'But you know him. So where would he go to hide? A friend? A girlfriend? Someone who'd help him out.'

'I ...'

Andy held up a finger. 'Take a minute to think before you answer, eh? Because I'm going to stop being nice to you if you say "I don't know" again.'

'But ...'

Andy covered Sanders' mouth and pressed down on the man's broken ribs. 'Now that has to hurt,' he said as Sanders howled into his hand. But the pain must've been too much for the man, as he suddenly went still and his eyes closed.

Shit. The idiot had passed out.

Releasing his grip on Sanders, Andy got out his little bag of cocaine. Dipping a key into it, he scooped up a small amount and then stuck the end of the key up Sanders' nostril, dumping the white powder. 'Have a whiff on that, lad.'

Andy squeezed the man's nostrils tightly together, covering his mouth once more. Unable to breathe, the man's body automatically started fighting for air. That was when Andy let go of the man's nose and Sanders sucked in air through his nose.

God only knew how much cocaine Sanders inhaled, but it was enough to get him to wake up, full of panic, fear and pain. Andy grinned. 'Where's Derrick?'

'He has a girlfriend ... mistress ... in Camberwell,' gasped Sanders. 'He might be there.'

'You see? You did know something. What's her name?'

'Tasha. Tasha Simcocks.'

'You got an address for her?'

'On the Maywood estate.'

Andy whistled. 'Not the best of addresses. You wouldn't be lying to me, would you?'

'No. I swear. If he's with anyone, it'll be her. I promise.'

'If you're lying to me,' Andy said, 'I'll be back — just like the fucking Terminator. And all the wonderful doctors and nurses won't be able to put you back together again. Comprendez?'

'Yes, yes,' Sanders said. 'I'm not lying.'

'Good. I'll leave you to get some rest now — but keep our little chat to yourself, eh? If you say anything to anyone. I'll feed you your balls.'

'I won't. I promise.'

Andy patted Sanders' cheek. 'Good lad. Now, I'll be seeing you.'

A minute later, Andy was out in the corridor, feeling good about life, and on his way down the stairs to the ground floor. He wished he had his car with him, but it was what it was. London wasn't exactly hard to get around without one.

He was in no mood for a bus or the tube though, so Andy hailed a black cab. 'Maywood estate,' he told the driver.

'You live there, mate?' the cabbie replied.

'Just visiting a friend,' Andy said, climbing in the back.

'They don't like strangers there,' the driver said. 'You sure you want to go there?'

'Just drive,' Andy said, sitting back, eyes closed. He could do this. He had to.

'It's your life,' the cabbie muttered, but he put the car in gear and drove off.

Andy pulled his phone out of his pocket and rang the nick. He didn't recognise who answered the phone and their name went in one ear and out the other but, after identifying himself, Andy asked for a DVLA check on a Tasha Simcocks, living on the Maywood estate, and he had a flat number a few seconds later.

He ended the call and stared out the window. It was only a ten-minute drive, past the best and worst of London. It was millionaires' houses one minute, then dangerous estates the next. No matter where, though, people packed the streets despite the hour. Ten o'clock and only just gone dark, the warmth of the day lingering while people drank outside pubs or bored kids hung around street corners looking for mischief, all under the orange glow of streetlamps and fluorescent shop signs.

For a moment, thoughts of his kids flashed through Andy's mind. Their lives would be ruined if he didn't sort things out. They'd lose the house and everything else. How'd he been so dumb? None of them deserved to have him for a dad. They were good kids, despite Andy's best efforts. God, he was proud of them. Loved them more than anything. How could he have let them down so much? What sort of role model was he turning out to be?

He shook the thoughts from his head. It wouldn't do himself any favours thinking about the kids. None whatsoever. He delved into his pocket for the wee baggie of cocaine and keyed a bump up each nostril.

'Hey!' the driver shouted. 'Don't do that in my cab. No drugs! I'll call the police if you do it again.'

'And you'll be going back to the hospital if you do,' Andy snarled, the cocaine already pounding through him. 'As a fucking patient. Just drive, eh?'

'Don't you threaten me,' the cabbie said.

'Fuck off, you gobshite.'

The driver served over to the side of the road and stopped by a Tesco express. 'Get out. Get out of my cab now!'

Andy couldn't believe it. The fucking cheek of the man. 'No, I will not,' he said through gritted teeth. 'You better drive me to the Maywood or you're going to be in a world of trouble.'

The driver was having none of it. 'No way, you junkie. Get out of my cab.'

Andy exploded. 'Who are you calling a junkie?' He smashed his fist against the plastic partition. 'Who. Are. You. Calling. A. Fucking. Junkie?' Again and again, he hammered the partition, shaking and rattling it but not breaking it. He fell back on the seat and started stomping on it with his feet. Bang. Bang. Bang. 'You better start driving or I'm going to kill you!' God, he really wanted to murder the man.

The driver got out his mobile. 'Get out now or I'm calling the police.'

'You shit! You wanker!' Andy screamed, spit flying. His fists pounded the partition. 'You fucking fuck!'

The driver dialled 999. 'Hello? Yeah, I need the police,' he said. 'I've got a madman in the back of my cab, threatening to kill me.'

Somehow, through Andy's drug-fuelled rage, a voice told him he had to get out of there. If the police turned up, he was screwed. There would be no talking his way out of it. 'Fuck you!' he screamed one more time, then opened the cab door, and all but fell out into the street, landing on his arse. The cab, wheels screeching, pulled out before the passenger door was properly shut, leaving Andy to pick himself up off the pavement.

Several people were watching and laughing from a bus stop, so he gave them the finger too before stomping off down the road. He'd gone maybe a hundred yards before he had to admit he didn't know where he was. Andy pulled out his phone and opened up Google Maps.

The Maywood estate was only two streets away. Andy rubbed his face and sniffed, trying to inhale any last lingering flecks of coke that might still be in his nose. He shouldn't do any more gear, even though he needed it to keep going. It was making it hard to think, his nerves raw and his temper frayed.

God, he hoped Morris was at his tart's place.

He set off once more, feeling jittery, grinding his teeth, and wanting to hurt someone. So, of course, his phone had to ring.

The caller ID said DEBBS WORK.

It was him. The bastard.

Andy didn't want to answer it, but knew he had to. He could feel the bastard's grip on his balls, squeezing tighter. Feeling sick, he accepted the call. 'Yeah?'

'Where are you?' The man's voice was as cold as granite.

'I'm on my way to the Maywood estate,' Andy said. 'Morris has a tart there. Sanders reckoned he might be holed up with her.'

'The Maywood, eh?'

'Yeah.'

'How far are you from it?'

'About two minutes.'

'When you get there, wait by the main doors. Someone will be along to see you.'

'Who?'

'You'll see.' The line went dead.

Andy was sweating like a paedophile in a clown's suit by the time he reached the Maywood. He blamed it on the summer weather, but it was more than likely down to the coke and the stress of it all. He was a fucking mess.

The Maywood was no better. The estate itself was a typical eyesore. Seven stories high, graffiti covered the ground floor walls, where a bunch of blue doors were all lined up from one end to the other and then repeated on every floor going up. No doubt some dick in the seventies designed the place in about ten minutes, working on a brief that said, 'Build as many homes as you can as cheaply as possible in the tightest space you can find.'

There was a new build opposite, mocking the state of the Maywood by showing what could be achieved with a little bit of effort — not that it was much more than a shithole itself.

Tasha Simcocks was on the fifth floor. Andy looked up, spotted her floor, then counted blue doors until he found hers. There was a light on in her front room, but lace curtains hid anything else from view. Still, that was promising. Very promising indeed.

But why did he have to wait for one of the bastard's crew to turn up? Why couldn't he just go in there and find out if Morris was there? Andy hated waiting. The street was too well-lit, and he stood out like a sore thumb. He might as well have been wearing a sign saying 'Suspicious.'

He rubbed his face and thought about doing another bump of

coke, but he was too wired as it was. Andy needed to keep his wits
about him if he was going to get out of this mess.

A kid on a bike caught his attention, whizzing out of the shadows,
cutting across the estate's parking area and headed straight towards
Andy. He couldn't have been more than eleven or twelve years old,
but he was decked out in thug fashion with a hood pulled up over his
head, so only the peak of his baseball cap jutted out. He was almost
too big for the bike he was riding, though, forcing his knees to stick
out at almost right angles.

The kid stopped by Andy. 'You the Fed?'

'What's it to you?' Andy said.

The kid reached inside his hoodie and pulled out a brown paper
bag. 'The man sent me. This is for you.'

Andy stared at the bag. 'What's in it?' he asked, even though he
didn't want to know.

The kid ignored the question. 'Take it.'

Andy took it. The moment the bag was out of the kid's hands, the
oik was off on his bike as fast as his little legs could pedal the damn
thing.

His heart hammering, sweat dripping off his brow, Andy opened
the paper bag and looked inside.

A gun stared back.

A revolver.

He reached in and took it out without thinking. The gun was
small but heavy, with a three-inch barrel. Andy recognised it. It was a
Ruger SP101, five bullets in the cylinder. They were big bullets, too.
357s by the looks of it. Magnum rounds. Killers. He put it back in the
back, wanting to puke. There was only one reason the bastard had
given him a gun.

His phone rang. It was DEBBS WORK. He answered, but couldn't
speak.

'You got it, then.' A statement, not a question.

'Yeah.'

'Can't have you going to see Morris with nothing but your cock in
your hand.'

'I thought I just had to find him for you.'

The man laughed. 'Yeah, but I thought, why waste time? You find him. You kill him. Make it look like an accident if you can. Blow his brains out if you can't.'

'I'm a cop. I can't kill him.'

'You had no problem killing Sonya.'

'What?'

'You murdered Sonya with that gun.'

'I didn't.'

'Oh yes, you did. After she tried blackmailing you with that silly video of hers. You shot her in the head with that gun.'

'I didn't.'

'Come now. You're the cop — as you keep telling me. You tell me what the police will think when they find her body, with a bullet fired from the gun in your possession, that has your fingerprints on it, and a video of you doing drugs and screwing her?'

'They'll think I did it.'

'Bingo. And if they think that, you might as well have done it — especially when my little friend, Marcus, sends them a picture of you standing outside the Maywood, holding the murder weapon.'

Andy's head shot up, eyes searching for the kid. It wasn't hard to spot him, sitting on his bike by a bench. The kid waved a phone at him, then rode off again.

'You bastard,' he breathed.

'You should really stop calling me names,' said the man, 'and do what I fucking tell you to do. Sort out Morris and no one will ever find Sonya's body and all the shit I have on you will go in the landfill with her. If you don't, if you're lucky, you'll end up in prison. If you're unlucky, you'll have your throat cut like dear old Tarik. Or your lovely wife, Debs, will.'

'Bastard,' Andy said, knowing there was no way the bastard was going to give up his hold on him, even if he killed Morris. No way on this earth. He was fucked.

'I can hear your little brain working frantically,' said the man.

'Don't waste your energy. There's only one thing you can do — so go do it.'

The line went dead.

Andy stared at the phone in his hand, the contents in the bag weighing heavy in his other hand. He should call Wise, confess everything. It had to be better than being that bastard's slave. Going inside had to be better than becoming a murderer.

But doing that would get his family killed.

Fuck.

He put his phone back in his pocket and entered the Maywood. The main lobby stunk of piss, mould and dope. Every surface was tagged and scrawled on. The mirror opposite the lifts had been battered by a brick or two. Only one of the overhead lights worked and even that was flickering off and on. It was like entering hell. How could people live in a place like this?

At least the lift worked. Andy got in, pressed the button for the fifth floor. The moment the doors closed, he took the gun out of the bag and stuck it into the top of his jeans, then pulled his t-shirt down to cover it. It was cold and uncomfortable against his skin, a reminder of what he had to do.

Dropping the bag on the ground, he watched the numbers of the floors light up as the lift creaked its way upwards. Knowing his luck, it'd break down and leave him trapped in there with a bloody murder weapon. Shit, why had the bastard killed Sonya? She might've been a bitch for filming him, but he knew she'd had no choice in that, just as he had no choice in doing what he was about to do. Sonya had been a good girl trapped in a shitty life. She didn't have to die for that.

The lift shuddered to a halt and, for a moment, Andy wished the cables would snap and it would plummet to the floor. An act of God that would be an act of mercy, putting him out of his misery.

But no, the doors creaked open, and Andy had no choice but to step out onto the landing. He fished out his little baggie of cocaine and keyed another bump up each nostril, then did a second round. He'd need all of it if he was going to kill someone.

11

Wise was in his tiny office, staring out the window at the night sky, all fed up. Despite everything, they had no leads on Morris' whereabouts. Not a single thing.

He got out his phone and called Callum.

'Yes, Guv?' the lad said.

'How are you and Brains getting on?'

'Morris hasn't been here yet. We spoke to the day manager, who didn't remember seeing Morris, and then we went through all the security footage for the afternoon just in case he'd missed something, but there was no sign of Morris. We've briefed the night manager to call us if he turns up, and now we're just sitting outside.'

'Give it another hour and then knock it on the head for the night,' Wise said. 'My gut says he would've turned up there already if there was something he needed from his lockup.'

'You sure?'

'Yeah. Better you two get some sleep. We'll have another long day tomorrow.'

'Cheers, Guv.'

Wise ended the call. He called Sarah next at MetCal. 'Any luck?'

'Nothing, Guv,' Sarah said. 'Maybe if we had an area to check but, at the moment, it's like trying to find a needle in a haystack.'

'Alright,' Wise said. 'I appreciate the effort. Go get some sleep.'

'See you tomorrow.'

He'd already sent Jono, Hicksy and Donut home. That just left Madge next door in MIR-One and Andy at the hospital. Andy could sort himself, but there was no point dragging Madge's misery out any longer. He got up from his chair, inched his way around his desk, and opened his office door.

Wise's desk phone rang before he could leave his office. He picked it up. 'DI Wise.'

'Guv, this is DC Swift,' a man's voice said. Wise knew the name vaguely but couldn't put a face to it. 'I've got a nurse on the blower from Lambeth Hospital. Says she wants to speak to DS Davidson's boss. That's you, right?'

'Yeah, that's me. Put her though.' A flutter of fear ran through Wise. Had something happened to Andy? There was a click on the line as the calls were connected. 'Hello, this is Detective Inspector Simon Wise.'

'Oh, hi,' a woman said. 'I'm Imelda Mathurin. I'm a staff nurse here at Lambeth Hospital.'

'How can I help you?'

'We have a Kevin Sanders in one of our private rooms. Someone had assaulted him earlier in the day.'

'That's right. I found him.'

'Well, I'm afraid to say he's been assaulted again.'

'What? How's that possible? I had an officer with him.'

'We discovered Mr Sanders a short while ago in a very agitated state. He claimed a man had tortured him, but he wouldn't say who. He also claimed the man had given him drugs when he'd passed out from the pain. We did a drug test and found small traces of cocaine in Mr Sanders' blood.'

'Cocaine?'

'That's right.'

'Where was my officer when all this was happening?'

'That's the thing,' said Mathurin. 'The only person to go into Mr Sanders' room all evening, other than my staff, was your officer.'

'What?' Wise felt the strength go from his legs. He sat on his desk.

'We checked the CCTV in the corridor outside Mr Sanders' room and the only person to go into and come out of the patient's room was your officer.'

Wise couldn't believe it. He felt like someone had punched him in the face. 'What about your staff?'

'We record all our visits on the patient's charts and none of my team entered the room unaccompanied. The only person who could have hurt Mr Sanders and given him cocaine is your officer — DS Andrew Davidson.'

'Thank you for letting me know. How is Mr Sanders now?'

'We've given him something for the pain and to counter the drugs. He's sleeping again now.'

'Okay. Thank you. I'll arrange for some uniform officers to stand guard outside his door with orders not to go in — just to make sure no one else tries to harm him.'

'Thank you, Inspector.'

Wise hung up the phone, shell-shocked. He couldn't believe it. Not Andy. Not his best friend — his best man at his wedding — his partner of God knows how many years. It couldn't be right but, somehow, Wise knew it was true.

Andy knew who was protecting Morris. He knew about Sanders and where he lived. Now this. The inside man wasn't Brains, it was Andy.

He picked up his desk phone and dialled DCI Roberts' office. She answered on the second ring. 'Yes?'

'It's Simon. I need to see you,' Wise said.

'Come up.'

A few minutes later, Wise had updated Roberts on everything. She looked as stunned as Wise felt.

'Have you spoken to Andy yet?' she asked.

'Not yet. I wanted to let you know first,' Wise said.

'Call him now. Don't let on you know anything. Just ask for an update, where he is — that sort of thing.'

Wise got out his phone, opened his contacts, scrolled through and found Andy's number. He hit dial. The phone rang and rang and rang until it eventually went to voicemail.

'That's not good,' Roberts said. Putting on her reading glasses, she started tapping away on her laptop. 'Let's see if there's any recorded activity from him in the past few hours.' She leaned forward to get a better look at her screen. 'What's this? He called in thirty minutes ago, asking for an address of a Tasha Simcocks.' Picking up a pen, she scrawled an address on a post-it note. 'Do you know who she is?'

'I've never heard of her,' Wise said. He looked at the address. 'The Maywood estate? Not the nicest of places.'

Roberts continued to tap away. 'Born December, 1982. No convictions. Not even an arrest.'

'Who is she? Some friend of Morris's? A girlfriend maybe?'

'Who knows, but it sounds like Andy has found some connection to Morris.'

Wise picked up the post-it note with the address. 'I'll go there now.'

'I'll arrange backup in case Morris is there.'

'Okay, but keep them on the ground. I'll speak to Andy by myself. Hopefully, I can stop him from doing something stupid.'

Roberts looked at him over the rims of her glasses. 'Unless he already has.'

Wise stood up. 'God, I hope not.'

He left Roberts' office and returned to the incident room where Madge was still working away. 'You in a hurry to go home?'

'I have no life, Guv,' Madge said. 'What do you need?'

'The shit has hit the fan and we need to stop it getting even more out of control.'

'Let me get my coat,' Madge said, standing up. 'Sounds just like the sort of job I love.'

Two minutes later, they were in Wise's knackered Mondeo, blue lights going, on their way to the Maywood estate. As he drove, Wise updated Madge on everything that had happened.

'He gave coke to a witness?' she spluttered.

'Looks like it,' Wise said. 'The nurse said he'd tortured Sanders for information.'

'Andy did?'

'Yup.' Even retelling for the second time didn't make it any easier to understand or accept.

'Fuck.'

'Yup.'

'And you reckon he dropped the close protection team in it with Selmani?'

'Only me and Andy knew where he was and who was looking after him. It seems bloody obvious now, but I still can't get my head around it.'

'They cut that poor sod's throat open,' Madge said. 'Because Andy dropped him in the shit?'

'I know,' Wise said, feeling sick. Andy was his friend. The godfather to his kids.

They blue lighted it straight down Kennington Road to the A3, then from there, they headed into Peckham via Brixton Road. Wise pushed the car as hard as he safely could, cutting a fifteen-minute journey into ten by the time they pulled into the car park of the Maywood estate.

Wise parked the Mondeo, looking up at the tower block. Was Andy there? God, he hoped they weren't too late.

'What floor's she on?' Madge asked as they climbed out of the car.

'Fifth,' Wise said, sprinting into the main building.

'The bloody lift better work,' Madge muttered. She punched the call button and, thankfully, the lift stirred into life. The doors opened painfully slowly, but then they were inside and the lift was climbing once more.

Wise watched the numbers light up above the door, anxiety rising with it. 'Dear God, let us be in time,' he muttered.

'Guv?' Madge said.

'Yeah?'

'Do you think we should've worn vests? What if someone's armed?'

Wise knew she really meant to say, 'What if Andy's armed?' That was a nightmare Wise didn't even want to contemplate.

The lift shuddered to a halt, and the doors opened on the fifth floor. 'Let's hope we don't need them,' Wise said, and stepped out onto the landing. 'It's too late to go back now.'

12

Andy's phone rang when he was halfway to Tasha Simcocks'
front door. He looked at the caller ID, thinking it would be
the bastard checking up on him, but it wasn't. It was Wise.
He stared at the phone, trilling away, unable to answer it, unable to
think of another lie to tell his friend, unable to think of a way to
pretend he wasn't falling into a deep, dark pit that there was no
getting out of. Of course, he'd been falling down that hole for a long
time now. Years, even. He was just at the bottom of it now.

At the end.

Fuck. Andy threw his phone over the balcony and watched it fall
to the car park below, all lit up, still ringing, until it smashed apart as
it hit the ground.

'Sorry, mate,' he said. 'I fucked it all up.'

He got the baggie out again. He poured what was left onto the
back of his hand and then snorted it as best he could. It would be all
over his face, but he didn't care. He was beyond caring about any of
that. Still, he rubbed his nose, sniffing all the more, trying to get as
much of it in him as he could. Its madness was all he had left. The
fuel to his fire, burning him down.

He marched down to Simcocks' flat and rang the doorbell. Every part of him twitched in a cocaine-induced mania. He chewed his lips, shuffled his feet, clenching and unclenching his grip on the pistol wedged into his jeans while staring at the front door, willing it to open.

'Come on. Come on. Come on,' he muttered to himself, getting more jittery. The clock was ticking. He needed to get this done. Sorted. Just do it. He sniffed, trying to breathe, feeling the drug racing through his brain, drying out his mouth, making it hard to think. 'Come on. Come on. Come on.'

Someone moved inside, walking towards the front door. 'Who is it?' a woman called out.

'Tasha Simcocks?' Andy said, loud enough to be heard through the door but hopefully not loud enough to disturb the neighbours.

'Who is it? What do you want? It's very late,' said the woman.

Late? It wasn't even 10:30, for God's sake. 'It's the police, Tasha. We need to speak to you.'

'Hold on.' Andy heard a chain being put on the door. It opened, stopping when the chain pulled tight and a sliver of woman's face appeared in the gap. Dark-haired, olive skinned, eyes bright and worried. Seeing Andy bouncing on her doorstep didn't put her any more at ease either. In fact, she looked petrified. 'Yes?'

Andy kicked the door with all his might.

The security chained snapped. The door flew open, sending Simcocks flying down the hallway. She hit a side table, then both fell to the floor. Andy stormed inside, pulling the gun out and aimed it at her head just as she started screaming. So much for not disturbing the neighbours.

'Where is he?' Andy screamed. Simcocks, dressed in a nightie and nothing else, tried scuttling away on her arse from him, but Andy went after her pretty damn quick. She got the message to stop wriggling when he pressed the gun against her forehead. 'Where's Morris?'

Her eyes flicked to a door to her right, and that was all Andy needed. He grabbed her by the hair, dragged her over to the door and kicked that in too. It burst open, the cheap lock a waste of time. It was the bedroom, decorated up in pink, with a big bed taking up most of the room. And there was Derrick Morris, holding the sheet up to his neck as if that would protect him. The twat.

Simcocks was still screaming, so Andy gave her hair another yank. 'Shut it.'

The command worked, and her cries became a whimper.

'I know you,' Morris said. 'You're a police officer.'

'Just get out of the bed and put some clothes on,' Andy snarled, waving the gun at the man.

Morris didn't move. 'I don't want to die.'

'It's too late for that. Now, get bloody dressed or I'll shoot you here and now.'

He watched Morris inch his fat body out of the bed, pick up his pants from the floor and slip them on while trying to keep his naked body covered by the sheet. Tears started running down Morris' cheeks as he put on his trousers. He looked over at Andy. 'Please.'

'Please what? You fucking piece of piss. You fucking worthless human being. Please what?' Andy jabbed the revolver at him. 'Come on. You're coming with me.' He walked backwards out of the bedroom, dragging Simcocks with him, but never taking his eyes or the gun off Morris. Out in the hallway, he hauled the woman to her feet.

She yelped with pain, but managed to stop herself from screaming again.

Morris, shirtless and barefooted, followed. 'Please, let her go. This has nothing to do with her. She knows nothing.'

'You shouldn't have got her involved then,' Andy said. 'In fact, you should've just kept your dick in your pants from the beginning and none of this would be happening. But you didn't and here we are. Now, get out.' He waved Morris towards the shattered front door with the gun.

'Where are we going?' Morris asked.

'Just get out.' Andy moved the gun, so he could press the barrel against Simcocks' temple. 'Or you can watch her die first.'

Morris held up both hands in surrender. 'Please — don't do that.'

He walked backwards to the front door, looking only when he nearly tripped on a bit of wood.

Andy manoeuvred Simcocks after him. 'I think he really likes you,' he whispered in her ear. 'Surprising, really, considering he normally only enjoys screwing whores.'

Simcocks whimpered in reply, but Andy didn't care. His blood was up now and everything was what it was. There was no stopping anything. No going back. No undoing what had already been done. What still had to be done.

He herded Morris and his woman down the landing to the lift and stairwell. Morris went to call the lift, but Andy waved him on. 'The stairs. Up.'

The stairwell stunk as bad as the rest of the estate. They walked up, past discarded cans, cigarette butts, shit graffiti, puddles of piss and a needle or two. Andy shook his head. How could people live like this? He'd be doing both of them a favour by killing them.

Morris stopped on the seventh floor, hand still in the air. 'Please let us go. We won't say anything. We'll disappear. You'll never see either of us again. I promise.'

'Keep going,' Andy said. 'The roof.'

There was a metal door on the next landing, but someone had broken the lock on it long ago and now it didn't even shut properly. It groaned as Morris pulled it open, revealing the night sky, a wash of cloud, illuminated by the glow of the city below.

Halfway out the door, Morris turned and tried one last time to beg for mercy. 'Please. Please. We're good people. Don't do this. You don't have to do this.'

'Yes, I fucking do!' Andy screamed. 'NOW GET OUT!'

Morris stumbled out onto the roof and Andy pushed Simcocks out after him. As he stepped onto the roof, he saw they weren't alone. A bunch of kids were in a corner, drinking alcopops and snogging. They screamed when they saw Andy with the gun.

'Go!' he shouted back and stepped aside so they could run down the stairs. He turned his head away from them, but he knew they'd seen his face. He knew they'd call the police.

He was screwed.

Morris and Simcocks held each other in their arms, both crying, both petrified. A part of him knew they didn't deserve to die like this, but neither did he deserve to be in the shit he was in. All their bad choices had put them up on that roof.

'Go on,' he said. 'Over there.' He pointed the gun to the side of the roof.

Neither Morris nor Simcocks moved. You didn't need to be a genius to guess what was going to happen once they got there. The four-foot wall that ran around the building's edge wouldn't stop them from going over.

'Why are you doing this?' Simcocks sobbed, bawling her eyes out.

'Because life's shit,' Andy said. He blinked and realised he was crying, too. Fuck. He didn't want to do this. He had to do this. 'Now, move your arses over there. We haven't got all night.'

As if to emphasise that point, he could hear wailing sirens from somewhere, coming their way as fast as they could, soundtracking all their dooms.

Andy pulled back the hammer on the revolver and pointed it at the lovebirds. 'Move!'

13

'Shit,' Wise said when he saw the broken door to Simcocks' flat. He glanced back at Madge. She shook her head. It wasn't what they wanted to see. What had Andy done? 'This is the police,' he called out. 'We're coming in. No one do anything stupid.'

With a nod to Madge, they both entered the flat.

The hallway was a mess. Bits of wood from the door were scattered everywhere and a side table had been overturned. Further down, another door had been kicked in. Wise glanced in, but it was empty. 'No one here,' he called out to Madge.

'Kitchen and living room are empty too,' she replied.

They met again in the hallway. 'The question is whether the place was empty when Andy got here, or has he taken Simcocks somewhere?' Wise said.

'Hello?' Wise and Madge turned to see a white-haired lady at the door, leaning on a zimmer frame. 'You police?'

Wise held up his warrant card. 'We are.'

'You got here quick. I only just called 999,' the woman said. She looked around. 'I would've thought there'd be more of you, though. What with the gun and all.'

'We're not here in response to your call,' Wise said. 'What gun?'

'The man who dragged that nice lady, who lives here, out onto the landing — he had a gun with him. I saw it.'

'The man — what did he look like?'

'He was white, tall, thin, bald. Looked crazy.'

That was Andy alright. 'How long ago was he here?'

'Maybe five, ten minutes,' the woman said. 'They went up the stairs.'

Wise looked at Madge. 'The roof.'

'We should definitely have worn vests,' Madge said, but she followed him anyway as he headed out of the flat.

'Best you stay inside your home,' Wise said to the woman as he passed her. 'Safer that way.'

'You don't think he'll come after me next, do you?' she called out after them as they ran down the landing to the stairs.

As they reached the stairwell, a bunch of kids came hurtling down from above. Wise grabbed one of them. 'What's going on? What's the rush?'

'There's a man on the roof with two others,' the kid said, trying to pull out of Wise's grip. 'He's got a pistol.'

Wise let him go and the kid didn't waste a second to sprint off after his friends down the stairs.

'If Andy's got a gun, we should call in Armed Response,' Madge said. 'Get a negotiator down here.'

'And what if he kills Simcocks and Morris while we do that?' Wise said.

'No offence, but I'd rather they get a bullet than me,' Madge said.

Wise nodded. 'You stay here. I'll go up. No point in both of us getting killed.'

Madge grabbed his arm. 'Guv, neither of us should get killed. Standard Ops says we call in the AROs in situations like this.'

'Andy won't shoot me,' Wise said, pulling his arm free. 'Make the call though — just in case I'm wrong.'

'Guv, don't,' Madge called out, but he was already climbing the stairs. By the time he reached the seventh floor, he could hear muffled voices from up above — someone shouting, others crying.

He turned the corner and saw the roof door wide open, London's sky beyond, warm air drifting down. There were sirens too, lots of sirens. The cavalry was on its way.

He took his time climbing the last few steps. The last thing he wanted to do was go bundling out onto the roof, spook Andy and get shot for his troubles.

'Why are you doing this?' a woman said. Simcocks.

'Because life's shit,' Andy said. His voice cracked raw with pain. 'Now, move your arses over there. We haven't got all night.'

Wise drew nearer to the door. He could see the rooftop, but there was no sign of Andy or the others yet.

'Move!' his friend shouted. His partner. His friend.

Wise wasn't too late. Andy hadn't killed anyone yet.

Yet. The word stuck in Wise's mind as he stepped through the doorway and onto the roof.

He saw them then. Morris, wearing only a pair of trousers, holding onto a woman who had to be Simcocks, both of them crying and on their knees, Andy behind them, a revolver in his hand, pointed at their heads.

'Andy!' Wise called out.

Andy flinched at hearing his name, then turned to face Wise.

'What the fuck are you doing here, Si?' Andy said, his eyes bulging, tears running down his face, all deathly white, flecks of powder on his nose and chin. The gun shook in his hand. 'You shouldn't be here.'

'Just trying to stop you from doing something stupid as usual,' Wise said, doing his best to sound calm. 'Why don't you put the gun down and let Derrick and Tasha go?'

Andy shook his head. 'I can't do that. They've got to die.'

'No, they don't,' Wise said, moving slowly towards Andy, hands held out in front of him as if trying to calm a wild animal. 'And you're not a murderer.'

'You'll think I am if he gets his way.'

'Who gets his way?'

'Him!' Andy shouted. 'The bastard.'

'I don't know who you mean,' Wise said. 'But it doesn't matter. None of it matters. Whatever you've done, whatever shit you're in, we can sort it out — as long as you put the gun down.'

'I can't, mate,' Andy said, sniffing. He rubbed his face. 'I can't. I've got to do this.'

Blue lights washed over the nearby buildings, strobing up from the ground as the sirens wailed below.

'Andy, you know what those lights mean,' Wise said. 'There's no getting away from this. Armed Response will be down there, too. If you're still holding that gun when they get up here, they won't hesitate. They'll shoot you.'

'Fuck!' Andy screamed. 'Fuck!' He looked around the roof, all crazy eyed, maybe hoping to spot a way out, an escape route off that roof. God, Wise prayed he didn't jump.

'Andy. Think of Debs and the kids,' Wise said, still moving closer, still trying to sound calm. 'Don't make this worse for them. Put the gun down.'

'I am thinking about them,' he cried, tears streaming now. He looked down at Morris and Simcocks. 'I am thinking about them.'

'Please, Andy. Listen to me,' Wise said. 'It's fine if you don't want to put the gun down, but let them go. Killing them will achieve nothing now. Selmani will go to prison and you'll be safe from him too.'

'Selmani? You think I'm worried about Selmani? He's nothing. Nothing! There's far worse people out there than Selmani.' Andy took a step back, all jittery and wired as hell. How much cocaine had the man taken?

'Whoever is making you do this, Andy,' Wise said, 'we can help you. Protect you.'

'Like we're protecting this fuck?' He jabbed the gun back against Morris' head.

'Give me the gun, Andy. Please — think of your wife. Your kids.'

'I am thinking of them!'

'Please, Andy. Before the AROs get here. Give me the gun.' Wise took a step towards his partner, hand out.

'Don't come any closer,' Andy cried, his eyes wide and bulging, burning cocaine bright. Sweat glistened across his face and soaked his t-shirt. He pressed the revolver against Morris' head, but Wise could see the shaking in his hand. 'Take another step and I'll shoot him.'

'Mate, please,' Wise said. 'I don't know why you're doing this, but we can sort it out. We can fix it — if you give me the gun. You're not a murderer.'

'You don't know what I am!' Andy said. He wiped his free hand across his face, rubbing the snot from his nose, blinking tears of his own away. 'I have to do this.'

A red dot danced across Andy's shoulders, seeking his head, finding its spot, stopping on his temple, dead still. An armed response officer in one of the neighbouring buildings had Andy in his sights, the laser targeting locked on a kill shot.

'No!' Wise shouted. He thrust both hands up in the air, turning, trying to see where the sniper was. 'Don't shoot! Don't shoot.'

Time stopped as Wise waited for the crack of a shot and the sight of Andy's brains punched from his skull. But no shot came. No one had given the order to terminate his friend. Someone still hoped Wise could stop this without bloodshed — for now. The clock was ticking, though. The order would come soon. No one would risk Andy killing Morris. How long did he have? Minutes? Seconds?

He turned back to his friend. 'The AROs have got you in their sights, Andy. Please give me the gun before it's too late. Think of Debs. Think of Katie and Mark.' Think of me, he wanted to say. He'd already lost his real brother, he couldn't cope with losing Andy too. 'Don't let them shoot you.'

'If I don't do this,' Andy said, 'he told me he'd kill them. I can't let that happen.'

'Who did?' Wise took another step forward.

'I'm sorry, Si,' Andy said. 'I'm sorry for ev—' His head lurched forward before Wise heard the crack. Time slowed as Andy tumbled forward, red mist leading the way, his brains and blood already splattered across the rooftop. He landed on the concrete with a wet thud and lay unmoving, his eyes open and fixed on Wise, a hole in the side of his temple where the red dot had been.

More AROs ran out onto the rooftop, all dressed in black, balaclavas covering their faces, bulletproof helmets on top of those, plus goggles despite the heat, Heckler and Koch MP5 machine guns in the ready position, shouting orders, looking for more threats, making sure Andy was dead.

The AROs got Morris and Simcocks to their feet and bundled them away to the stairs. They picked up Andy's gun, made it safe, and bagged it. They checked Andy, shouted that the target was dead.

Then an ARO was saying something to Wise, but Wise couldn't understand him, couldn't reply, couldn't move. All he could see was the jerk in Andy's head as the bullet struck him, the shape of his mouth as his last breath left his body, and the look in his eyes as he fell, accusing Wise.

More people came out onto the roof. More police. An ambulance crew.

Someone put a tinfoil blanket over Wise's shoulders. Said more words he couldn't understand.

Madge appeared, hand over her mouth, staring at her dead colleague, her dead friend, then at Wise.

Wise felt the judgement in her eyes. The condemnation. He was their leader. He should've stopped this from happening.

Wise couldn't comfort her, couldn't say anything that would make this horror any better. He couldn't even blink.

All he could see was Andy dying.

Andy dead.

Dear God.

Four days later

14

Wise sat in Roberts' office. Suit on, shirt starched, tie done tight. Immaculate. His face a mask. 'The Selmani trial has gone well. Morris was a perfect witness.'

On the other side of her desk, Roberts nodded. 'I heard, but that's not why I wanted to see you.'

Wise stiffened. He didn't want to have this conversation. He didn't want to talk about what happened.

'Professional Standards will get in touch with you next week,' Roberts said. 'They're going to be looking into Andy and what happened.'

Wise blinked. *The gun shot loud in his head, the bullet punching Andy off his feet, his brains decorating the rooftop.* 'Right. Of course.'

'Specialist Crime and Operations are also involved,' Roberts continued. 'They're interested in this other man Andy spoke of — the one he claimed ordered him to assassinate Morris. They're handling the murder of Tarik Gardner, too.'

'I don't know anything more than what I've put in my report,' Wise said. 'Andy never mentioned a name — just that it was a man.'

Roberts looked away for a moment, her own discomfort obvious. 'And you never suspected Andy was doing this person's bidding?'

'No.'

'What about the drugs?'

'No.'

Roberts raised an eyebrow. 'No?'

'No,' Wise repeated. 'I knew he liked a drink. Some days he came in hungover or looking like he hadn't slept but I never thought he was using anything.'

'But you knew he was sleeping around.'

'Not the same thing.'

'I'd say someone constantly cheating on their partner would suggest they were lacking the morals for this job.'

'You've got to be joking,' Wise said. 'If we disqualified people from service based on adultery, then we're in real trouble.'

'I know. I know,' Roberts said. 'I'm sorry. This is hard on all of us. Everyone liked Andy — myself included. Have you seen his family?'

'A few times. They're devastated, as you can imagine. They don't understand any of this either.'

'His poor wife.' Roberts shook her head. 'It's going to get worse for them though, I'm afraid.'

It took everything Wise had to keep his face still, his mask intact. 'How?'

'The body of a prostitute was found a couple of days ago,' Roberts said. 'She'd been shot in the head.'

'What's that got to do with Andy's family?'

'Ballistics matched the bullet that killed her to Andy's gun.'

'Shit.'

'She also had a phone on her that contained a film of her and Andy having sex together and doing drugs.'

I'm sorry, Si,' Andy says. 'I'm sorry for ev—'

Wise gritted his teeth. He had to stay in control. 'Right.'

'The tape alone would be motive enough for Andy to kill her,' Roberts said.

'He wouldn't have—' Wise stopped himself from saying anything else. He had no idea what Andy would've done or not done. His best friend, his partner, was a mystery to him. 'It's a sad business.'

'Madge has put in a transfer request.'

'I don't blame her.'

Madge appears, hand over her mouth, staring at her dead colleague, her dead friend, then at Wise.

Wise feels the judgement in her eyes. The condemnation. He's their leader. He should've stopped this from happening.

'And what about you, Simon?' Roberts asked. 'How are you holding up?'

Andy lies unmoving, his eyes open and fixed on Wise, a hole in the side of his temple where the red dot had been.

'I'm fine,' Wise lied, fists clenched out of sight behind the desk. He could feel the cracks spreading day by day. Feel the pain growing deeper.

Like an unwanted friend come to stay once more.

THANK YOU

Thank you for reading *Dead Man Running,* a Detective Inspector Simon Wise thriller. It means the world to me that you have given your time to read one of my tales. It's your support that makes it possible for me to do this for a living, after all.

Keep reading for the first few chapters of *Rich Men, Dead Men,* the first full-length DI Simon Wise thriller and find out what happens next.

Thank you once again!

Michael

Tuesday, 13th September

15

Mark Hassleman leaned over the coffee table and sprinkled more cocaine onto the glass surface. He let a nice little pile fall from the little plastic bag — but not too much. There wasn't much left, and he'd already had more than enough Charlie for the night. More than enough to last a lifetime if truth be told, but Mark tried not to think about that too much. After all, what was the point of being a tech multi-millionaire if he couldn't enjoy the simple little pleasures in life?

Not that a five hundred pound a day cocaine habit was a simple pleasure. It was a hard-earned extravagance. What was it Robin Williams had said? Cocaine was God's way of letting you know you had too much money? He'd been damn right about that.

Back in Hassleman's college days, he'd thought only movie stars and rock singers did cocaine. Not people like him. Not the nerds, geeks, and the socially awkward. What would his friends from back then say now if they saw him like this? Hunched over a table of powder, a half drunk bottle of whisky by his side, shut off from the world with the curtains drawn. They'd not think he was living the dream. They'd be unimpressed. Disappointed. Shocked.

From *Wired* to wired.

But who cared? He didn't. Hassleman was a million miles away from them. He wasn't just living in a different world; he was in a different stratosphere. He was the rich and famous now. And he was only too aware of the irony that his fame, his fortune, had come from an app designed to get people laid, created by a man who once upon a time couldn't get lucky to save his life.

Hassleman laughed at that. Necessity was the mother of invention, after all.

Hassleman picked up his black AmEx card and began delicately shaping the powder into lines. Small, sensible, thin ones because he was going to make this pile last the rest of the night. He certainly wouldn't finish the rest of the bag. He definitely wouldn't call for more. Hassleman had told Ivan as much when he'd dropped off the last delivery. Told him not to come back that day even if Hassleman called. Not even if he begged. Hassleman had to have some self-control left, prove to himself that he wasn't an addict, that he was doing all the blow for fun, not need.

His hand carved and re-carved the lines, already making the sensible lines into something more ... impressive. Bigger. Bolder. Not too much, but enough. To do less was a waste of time.

Soon, his sensible little lines had merged into three long train tracks but Hassleman pretended not to notice, still believing he was going to make it last, that what was on the table was all he'd have and no more. Believing his own lies. Fooling himself.

He rolled up the hundred-dollar bill he kept just for snorting coke with, stuck it in his nostril and bent down once more, breathing in, racing along one line, then swapped the note to his other nostril and went to work on the second line, struggling a bit more this time, his nostril already clogged with everything he'd stuffed up it earlier, but he preserved.

God, it stung. He squeezed his nose together, making sure he didn't sneeze as he felt the drip run down the back of his throat, felt the coke kick in, a dull thump instead of the roar it'd been at eleven that morning when he'd started. All because he'd been bored.

Not that he needed much of an excuse these days.

He leaned back on the leather sofa, mind racing, going nowhere fast. Should he stay in or should he go out? Maybe make some calls. Call some people. Have some drinks. More drinks. He'd sunk most of a bottle of whisky, as it was. He didn't need more.

Or did he? He was in now. Settled. He wasn't even sure what time it was. The curtains were closed all day, cutting off the world. Just the way he liked it. Who knew what everyone else was up to? They wouldn't be on his wavelength even if he did meet up with them.

Then it would be awkward. Uncomfortable. He certainly didn't need anyone judging him and ruining his high.

Better he stay in. Stay alone. He preferred it that way, anyway.

Porn played on the eighty-inch TV that filled the far wall of the living room. Bodies doing this and that in glorious 4k. Ultra-hard, utterly depraved. Not that it meant anything. Not that it turned him on. He didn't know why he was watching it. If he was watching it. Why did he have it on? When did he turn it on?

He rubbed his face, feeling hot, feeling clammy, then downed his glass of whisky and poured another. He needed the booze to take the edge of the coke, smooth out the jitters, quieten the crazy thoughts.

He muted the porn and turned on some music. Stormzy thundered from the stereo. That was better. The bass was deep and loud. Pulsing through him. Shaking the walls. Pounding in time with his heart. A hundred beats a minute. Heart attack time. Maybe he should turn that down. He didn't want anyone coming around to complain. Not now. Not when he was like this. Feeling good. Feeling electric.

Living the fucking dream.

He bent down and inhaled the third line. His last line. The last of the night. Thank God for that. A few more drinks and he could call it a night. Pop a xanax. Get some sleep. He'd feel better in the morning. Yeah, early night.

How boring did that sound?

The night was just getting started. He was just getting started.

Hassleman looked at the dregs left in the bag. It wasn't a lot. Maybe enough for one more line. A small one. Maybe he should get tomorrow's supply in tonight? Have it ready for when he needed it? Ivan wasn't a morning person, after all. What drug dealer was? It was better to have it and not need it than to need it and not have it. Or something like that.

He picked up his phone, opened WhatsApp, clicked on the conversation with Ivan. It was full of the usual drug dealing drivel. Bad code that wouldn't fool an imbecile, let alone the police. Still, it was how it was done. Expected. Everyone played the game.

He had to focus on the screen and concentrate on what he typed. 'Mate, decided to go to the party after all. Can you drop five VIP tickets off at my place?'

Ivan pinged back two seconds later. 'LOL. I thought you weren't going to call me?'

'How long?' Hassleman messaged back.

'Ten minutes.'

Thank God for that. Hassleman put the phone down and picked the bag up, emptying the last of its contents on the table. He'd made the right call, making the call. Who was he kidding? The night was young, and he was king of the fucking world. Even Zuckerberg hadn't made his first million as quick as he had. Now he was chasing his first billion three years on. After that? Who knows what he could do? What he could achieve?

Maybe he'd be president of the United Fucking States. Make his mom proud of him at last. The bitch.

He sprinkled the last the specks of Charlie over the table, free of the pretence of restraint. Picked up the note. His hundred-dollar bill. Down he went, as quick as he could. One snort and it was gone. That was it.

Finito.

Until Ivan arrived.

Hassleman wiped his nose, sniffing more, aware of flakes falling from his nose, wasting what was there. He tipped his head back, letting gravity help him instead of rob him of his precious drugs.

God, what was he doing? It was madness. Stupid. Why had he done all the coke? Why had he called Ivan for more? He should message him back. Cancel the order. He didn't need it. Didn't want it. He had to have some control. He wasn't an addict after all. It was just fun. Too much fun once. Not enough now. Never enough.

The doorbell rang.

Ivan.

That was quick.

Oh well. Ivan was there now. The drugs were there. He might as well pick them up. It'd be rude not to.

Hassleman jumped to his feet, then needed a moment to steady himself. He blinked, eyes wide, trying to focus, a little voice whispering it was a bad idea while another shouted it was a bloody good one.

It was hard work walking from the living room to the front door. He was drunker than he thought, definitely more wasted. It took him so long, Ivan rang the doorbell again. Impatient bastard. Hassleman thought about keeping him waiting even longer, teach him a lesson, leave him out on his doorstep to show him who was boss, who was in charge.

But who was Hassleman kidding? He wanted Ivan inside, off his doorstep, out of sight of his neighbours and Ivan's drugs out of his pocket and into his nose.

He checked himself in the mirror by the door, making sure he had no cocaine on his face. Nothing to give away what he'd been doing all day, just in case it wasn't Ivan. He didn't want to frighten the neighbours. But who else would it be? Only Ivan. Only his drugs. No one else called.

Sucking his teeth in anticipation, Hassleman opened the big, black front door.

But it wasn't Ivan standing there. It wasn't his drugs.

It was a man wearing a motorbike helmet, and he had a gun pointed at Hassleman's face.

'No,' said Hassleman, putting up his hand, as if that could stop a bullet.

Wednesday, 14th September

16

Wise tried not to yawn as he reached Ladbroke Grove and failed miserably. The last thing he'd needed was a call out at 1:30 in the morning. Not that he'd been asleep. He didn't do much of that anymore. Not since …

'I'm sorry, Si,' Andy says. 'I'm sorry for ev—'

He blinked the memory away and concentrated on where he was. Ladbroke Grove. It was a place he always associated with The Clash, his dad's favourite band — not that it bore any resemblance to when the punk band had called it home. The working class was long gone, replaced by big money.

That was never more true than in Elgin Crescent. It was one of the most expensive streets to live in London and that was really saying something these days. It certainly wasn't the sort of place where people got murdered.

Police barriers stopped traffic entering or leaving the street under the watchful eye of two uniformed officers. One came over with a clipboard to check Wise's ID card. After noting his details down, the officer went back to move the barrier enough to allow his car through.

There was a row of Georgian terraced houses on one side of the street, some of which were converted into apartments, but each one had to be worth several million pounds each. On the other side, the prices of the detached Georgian mansions had to stretch into the tens of millions.

Wise didn't need to be much of a detective, though, to know where the crime scene was. Flood lights illuminated a white awning over the entrance to one of the mansions two-thirds of the way down on the right-hand side of the street. Scene Of Crime Officers — SOCOs — were going in and out in their white forensics suits, all hooded up, while the road outside the house looked like a police station car park. Wise passed three patrol vehicles, a forensics van, and two unmarked cars before he found a spot to park his knackered old Mondeo, blocking a top-of-the-range Land Rover and a Jag. A quick glance down the rest of the residents' cars confirmed that most of the residents' vehicles had at least a hundred grand price tag attached to them, but it was that kind of neighbourhood.

So very different from where Wise lived.

He sat for a moment, watching the goings on. He spotted DS Roy Hicks on the pavement, head down, shoulders all hunched up in his crumpled raincoat, hands deep in his pockets. Waiting where Andy should've been waiting.

A red dot dances across Andy's shoulders, seeking his head, finding its spot, stopping on his temple, dead still.

Wise closed his eyes and composed himself, fighting the cracks, smothering the pain. He looked in the rear-view mirror and made sure his face gave nothing away. This was no time for memories or ghosts. He had a job to do.

It was all he had left.

His face a mask, he grabbed his suit jacket and phone off the passenger seat and got out. The phone went into his pocket and then he slipped the jacket on, taking a second to smooth the front and button it up. Only then did he walk over to his colleague.

'Hicksy,' Wise said.

'Guv,' Hicksy replied. His voice was so flat he might as well have been addressing a stranger instead of his boss for the past five years. That was another fallout from Andy's betrayal and death. Wise's team had lost all the closeness that had made them so effective, their faith in each other.

If Wise wasn't feeling as out of place as the rest of them, he might've known what to say to repair the damage and bring everyone back together, but he nodded towards the house. 'What happened?'

'Officers responding to a 999 call found a man shot dead on his doorstep at approximately 11:25 this evening,' Hicksy said. His hair was cut so short it barely existed and he had broken his nose so many times that it zigzagged down the middle of his face like a lightning bolt. The shadow cast from his wild eyebrows hid his deep-set eyes, making him look more tired than Wise felt.

'We know who he is?' Wise asked.

'The house belongs to a Mark Hassleman, twenty-eight. Apparently, he's the social media guru who invented the Sparks dating app.'

'I've heard of him. "Britain's Bill Gates."'

Hicksy nodded. 'That's the one, Guv.'

'Anyone else in the house at the time?'

'No, he was alone, as far as we know. The uniforms who responded to the 999 call had a quick look around. There're traces of cocaine on the coffee table and porn's playing on his TV, but that's it.'

'A party for one, then?'

'Looks that way, Guv.'

'Who's the Home Office pathologist on call tonight?'

'Harmet Singh.'

'That's good. Is she here yet?'

'Got here about twenty minutes ago.'

'What about our team?'

'Jono's talking to their neighbours. School Boy's inside having a look around and Sarah's headed to Kennington. She's getting the street CCTV footage requested — not that there's going to be a lot.

Cameras only cover the crossroads with Kensington Park Road at one end and Ladbroke Grove at the other. The rest of the street is a blank.'

'Some houses must have cameras — if not all of them.' Wise said. 'Action someone with getting copies of anything they might have filmed.'

'Will do,' Hicksy said. 'I told the rest of the team to be ready for you at 8:30 a.m. for the DMM.' The Daily Management Meeting was the heart of any investigation for Wise. Solving a crime was like putting together a jigsaw puzzle, getting small pieces of information and slotting them together bit by bit, until the overall picture appeared. The DMMs were the place where he assembled that picture from everything he and his team uncovered, where he could create order from chaos.

'Good,' Wise said. 'Now, let's see who got killed.'

At the forensics van, Wise and Hicksy gave a SOCO their IDs to check. In return, the officer gave them each a suit with a hood to put, plus gloves and coveralls for their shoes. The outfits were supposed to be one-size-fits-all, but Wise was a big man, and every time he put one of the suits on, he tested the sizing description to its limits. In fact, on more than one occasion, the suit had ripped apart, much to everyone else's amusement.

Dressed, they moved from the forensics van to the house, where the scene guard signed them into the logbook.

A white tent covered the short path up to the front of the house and treads were in place along the side of the house steps for the officers to walk on to preserve the crime scene and any evidence that the killer might've left behind.

SOCOs were scuttling here and there, looking for anything out of place that might provide a clue to who killed Hassleman. And, of course, there were SOCOs working just inside the doorway, examining the body. Even from the bottom of the steps, Wise could see the bare feet of the victim sticking up and, over the heads of the working SOCOS, the blood and brains that covered the wall behind.

Andy's head jerks as the bullet hits him. Red mist erupts from the other side of his head. His brains hit the concrete roof a heartbeat before Andy's body.

Wise clenched his fists, burying the memory. This wasn't the time. He concentrated on his breathing, forced his legs on, acted like everything was alright. He couldn't let anyone see any weakness. Not Hicksy, not the SOCOs. He was in control.

With a deep breath, Wise went to look at the dead man.

17

As Wise and Hicksy reached the top of the steps to the Georgian mansion, one of the suited figures examining the body looked up, as if sensing they were there.

'Hello, Inspector,' Harmet Singh said. She was a rising star in the forensics world and had never failed to impress Wise when they'd previously worked together. She had a good sense of humour, too, and liked a bit of banter. That was always a good thing. Especially when things were as bad as they often were.

'Doctor,' Wise said. 'What brings you out here tonight?'

'You know me, can't resist a corpse in the middle of the night.' Singh stood up, arching her back slightly. She wasn't much over five feet in height — at least a good foot smaller than Wise — and she was drowning in her one-size-fits-all forensics suit.

Wise nodded at the body. 'He's definitely dead, then?'

'As some of his brains are covering the wall and floor behind him, I'd say so,' Singh said.

Wise ran his eye over the corpse. The man was wearing dark blue jeans and a black t-shirt with a smiley face on it. His head turned to the left, so the damage by the bullet was out of sight but, as Singh had said, most of his brains lay in a dark red pool of blood behind him and decorated the wall on the other side of the hallway.

He'd died just like Andy.

God, he wanted to be sick. He shouldn't be there, working this case. Shouldn't be working at all. 'How many times was he shot?' he said, trying to focus.

'There are two bullet wounds,' Singh said. 'One to the hand, one to the face. However, we've only recovered one bullet so far.' Singh pointed to the bloody wall. 'From amongst that mess.'

'One bullet, two wounds?'

'He could've put his hand up as they shot him.'

'What? To stop the bullet?'

'It's instinctive. It happens more often than you'd think.'

Wise glanced down the corridor to the main part of the house. The wooden floorboards looked spotless. 'No bloody footprints.'

'It doesn't look like the killer entered the house after they killed the victim,' Singh said. 'But we're checking everything.'

'So the motive wasn't robbery then?' Wise said, more to himself.

'Again, you're the detective, Inspector,' Singh said. 'I'll leave that sort of thing up to you to work out.'

Wise stared at the body. 'Someone rang the doorbell. Hassleman answers it. They shoot him, then walk away. No messing about.' Just like the AROs did with Andy.

'Pissed off boyfriend or husband?' Hicksy suggested. 'Maybe he hooked up with someone he shouldn't have done.'

'Maybe,' Wise said. 'And it's definitely Hassleman who's dead, Doctor? No chance it's a house guest or something like that?'

'He had a driver's licence in his wallet,' Singh said. 'The picture matches.'

'That's something, at least,' Wise said. 'Still, we'll need someone to formally identify him.'

'I'll look into next of kin,' Hicksy said.

'Good. Let's have a nose around inside,' Wise said.

'I'd rather you didn't traipse past here just yet. There's a private garden around the corner, shared by the residents,' Singh said. 'You can access Hassleman's private garden from there and then get into the house via the back door.'

'Thank you, Doctor,' Wise said. 'Let us know when you know anything.'

'I'll be in touch,' Singh said. 'The PM should be first thing in the morning.'

Wise turned around and headed back down the steps, Hicksy following. They both removed the blue foot coverings that prevented their shoes from leaving any marks, then headed to the corner of Kensington Park Road, to the entrance to the private park; a gate set in a row of iron railings.

Wise looked around and quickly spotted the CCTV cameras affixed to the lampposts and traffic lights. 'Good camera coverage here.'

Hicksy nodded. 'Shame they put all the bloody cameras here and not in Elgin Crescent. Could've made our job easier.'

After showing their warrant cards again to the uniforms manning the entrance to the park, they entered the gardens and immediately the world grew darker, away from the street lamps and under the trees. The rear of Hassleman's was easy to spot, though, illuminated by more police lights.

Another uniform waited under the lights by a smaller gate, set in a low wall. On the other side was a narrow, well-tended garden.

Both put back on the plastic coverings over their shoes and made their way across more metal treads to the back door.

'I wonder why they shot him on the front doorstep?' Hicksy said. 'The killer could've snuck through the back gardens and entered the house this way. No one would've seen them entering. They could've killed Hassleman without fear of interruption and the body would've gone undiscovered for days, depending on when anyone was expecting to see Hassleman next. Plenty of time to get away.'

'From what I could tell, the CCTV had pretty much all the park entrance covered,' Wise said, 'whereas the front of the house is a complete blind spot. That's reason enough. And what if the killer wanted the body found? There's a message in killing a well-known man like Hassleman. Someone who's rich. Successful.'

'A professional hit?'

'Could be. You don't get this sort of money without pissing someone off along the way — or having someone want what you have.'

They entered the house into the kitchen. It was a decent size and well-equipped, but it didn't look like Hassleman was much of a home cook. Empty delivery boxes were piled up next to a full bin and there were several empty pizza boxes lying around on the countertops, along with empty beer cans, wine bottles and whisky bottles.

'Bloody hell. Looks he had a party after all,' Hicksy said.

'Or the cleaner's been on holiday,' Wise said, looking at the kitchen table covered in unopened mail. 'Maybe his PA too.'

'Maybe he was just a slob,' Hicksy said. 'I've always thought these boffins weren't normal.'

They walked out of the kitchen into the living room. Judging by the smell in the room, Hicksy was probably right about Hassleman being a slob. The room stunk of stale air, mixed with body odour and alcohol.

Someone had paused the porn on the big TV, leaving a still image on the screen of a woman hard at work on her male counterpart. The picture was so bright that Wise had to squint as he tried to look around the room. 'I think we can turn off the television now,' Wise said to the SOCOs in the room. 'We're not immature teenagers, after all.'

'Sorry, Guv.' A SOCO picked up a remote control that was already bagged up and pressed the power button. The screen went dark.

'That's better,' Wise said. There was a black leather sofa positioned to face the TV, with a kidney-shaped, glass coffee table in front of that, covered with the detritus of Hassleman's evening entertainment. There was a near empty bottle of scotch next to a tumbler with a mouthful left in it and a mobile on one side while the other half of the table had smears of white powder next to a rolled up dollar bill, a black American Express card and several, small empty plastic baggies that, no doubt, once were full of cocaine. 'He was really going for it.'

Hicksy nodded. 'Twenty-eight years old with more money than God? I think I might lose the plot too.'

'Such a waste.'

'Maybe his death was a drug deal gone wrong?'

'Maybe,' Wise said. 'I'm not sure, though. Hassleman would've been the best sort of customer — a heavy user with lots of money. He's not going to argue about money or try to stiff his dealer.'

'That amount of coke's enough to send anyone nuts, though,' Hicksy said. 'If he wasn't alone and Hassleman started arguing with whoever he was with ... Things get out of hand. The friend storms out, Hassleman follows, calling them every name under the sun. The friend turns around, pulls a gun and shoots him on the doorstep.'

The rest of the room was sparsely decorated; a couple of uncomfortable armchairs, an arc light dangling over the sofa and table and an expensive-looking rug covering the centre of the floor. Art covered several of the walls. Wise wasn't an expert, but even he recognised some pieces. Either Hassleman had great taste or he had a buyer who knew their stuff. 'Whatever happened, it definitely wasn't a robbery. The art in here has to be worth millions on its own.'

'Guv?'

Wise turned to see DC Callum Chabolah standing in the doorway. He was twenty-three and relatively new to the team, joining a month or two before Andy ... No, Wise didn't want to think about that.

The others called Callum 'School Boy,' on account of the fact he was still a trainee, doing his detective exams, but they just wished they had his energy. The lad was around five foot eight, with a slim build only young people can have and yet not appreciate. He wore dark jeans, a black sweater and a dark green bomber jacket, his hair cut with a fade. 'His office is upstairs, Guv. It's like something out of a spaceship.'

'Show me,' Wise said.

Callum led Wise and Hicksy up the narrow stairs to an equally dark and dingy upstairs. The first room off the stairs was a bedroom that had been converted into an office, but that seemed an inadequate way to describe the room. It looked more like a military command centre with nine monitors stacked in rows of three above the desk, each one bigger than most people's home televisions. A screensaver of a flame spark danced between the screens in a hypnotic pattern. There was an illuminated, curved keyboard on the desk, next to a wireless mouse and a trackpad and pen, plus more signs of white powder. The computer hard drive was in a monstrous tower next to the desk.

'Fucking hell. What did he need all these monitors for?' Hicksy said.

Wise walked over to the window. The shutters hadn't been opened for a long time. 'Get the tech bods on this tomorrow along his phone downstairs. I want to see his emails and messages, who he was talking to and what was being said. The guy was a tech genius, so there's a good chance we'll find a motive and maybe even a suspect in his hardware.'

'Will do, Guv,' Callum said.

'Is the main bedroom next door?' Wise asked.

'Yeah, Guv. It's a bit of a mess, too.' Callum led them back out into the hall and into the next room. It took up the rest of the second floor with windows that overlooked the gardens, but again shutters closed off the view. The bed was king-sized and unmade, with half the sheets lying on the floor, along with a good few days' worth of clothes strewn everywhere.

'Definitely a slob,' Hannah said, wrinkling her nose.

Wise peered into the ensuite bathroom. Towels littered the floor there as well and a tube of toothpaste, squeezed to death, was next to the sink. Wise checked the cabinet above the sink and found at least a dozen prescription pills bottles, some fuller than others. 'Looks like Hassleman liked his prescription drugs, too,' Wise said. 'They're all prescribed by the same doctor — a Doctor Onylil, Harley Street. There's some anxiety meds, and about three different brands of sleeping tablets.'

Hicksy peered over his shoulder. 'How did he get any work done if he was off his head all the time?'

'How many functioning alcoholics have you known over the years?' Wise said. 'Maybe he used these to balance the various drugs out, so he felt whatever he considered normal.'

'Can't be a kosher doctor, though, dishing all these out,' Hicksy said.

'Let's add Doctor Onylil to our list of people to talk to.'

They moved on. The walk-in wardrobe looked like a hurricane had ripped through it. Trainers lay half in and half out of boxes and clothes lay here and there or dangled off shelves; mainly t-shirts of various colours and jeans of every style.

'I don't think you and Hassleman would've gotten on,' Hicksy said. 'Not a suit in sight.'

'I think I'd object to the drugs before I worried about his wardrobe,' Wise said, looking over Hassleman's clothes. It wasn't as if Wise never wore jeans and t-shirts himself, but he could never bring himself to wear them to work. He might not have to wear a uniform anymore, but he found a comfort in having one still. Even more so now. A sharp suit hid the cracks. His dad had taught him that. "Shoes always polished. Shirt always starched. Suit pressed. World's already full of bums. You don't need to be one."

They moved through the rest of the house, but every other room looked unused simply by the fact they were clean and tidy. Hassleman seemed to only use the kitchen and living room downstairs and his office and bedroom upstairs.

It was gone 3 a.m. when Wise called it a night. 'So what do you think?' he asked as they walked outside into the bitter night, a drizzle of rain falling.

'I think Hassleman got rich too quickly,' Hicksy said, 'and if someone hadn't shot him, he'd have been dead of an overdose sooner rather than later — but there's a lot to look at. Who gets his money, first and foremost?'

'Callum?'

'I think maybe it was the drugs,' the lad said. 'He could've found a new dealer and pissed off the old one, or maybe he was trying to buy wholesale instead of retail?'

Wise nodded. He nearly turned around to ask Andy for his opinion before remembering he wasn't there.

Andy tumbles forward, red mist leading the way, his brains and blood already splattered across the rooftop.

'We've certainly got lots to look into — his love life, his finances, his business dealings and his drug habits. Let's pull his life apart and see what drops out. No one this wealthy gets murdered by accident.'

They returned their suits to the forensics van. After saying good night, Hicksy and Callum left Wise standing alone. He stood staring at the front of Hassleman's house, not caring about the rain, picturing Hassleman at the front door, a gun in his face. Did he even know he was about to die?

Had Andy?

He climbed into the Mondeo, feeling exhausted. It'd been a long day, in an already long week of an even longer month. Ever since that night, he was finding it harder and harder to pretend to be the man he used to be.

Slipping the Mondeo into gear, he made his way to the Ladbroke Grove exit, merged into the night traffic, and headed home. He watched the streets as he drove, London coming more alive as he left the more wealthy, residential areas. There were a good few drunks falling out of clubs, trying to hail cabs or stagger off to somewhere else, eager to carry on despite it being a school night. Then there were the homeless, curled up in shop doorways, trying to sleep or shoot up or drink their way to numbness. Others wandered past on their way home, knackered after a long night's work, caught up in their own worries and ignoring the world. Delivery people dropped off stock for the next morning while the all-night takeaways and cafes blazed neon out into the night, flogging greasy food to the night crowd.

It was strange, but this was the London Wise loved. At night, the city felt more real to him, stripped of the respectability that drew the tourists by the thousands during the day. It brought back memories of running wild with his brother, out after dark when they shouldn't be, getting in trouble, drinking underage, having fights, having laughs, trying to pull, sometimes getting lucky, sometimes not.

He'd not thought about his brother in a while, hadn't spoken to him in even longer, and that had been ... not good. God, he missed him. Missed Tom. Missed what they had back then. They'd been inseparable ever since they'd shared a womb together, together until that night forced them apart. That night and the trial and the prison sentence.

Their relationship wasn't the same after that. Couldn't be, no matter how much Wise had wished it so. But, even now, he wondered if it had to get as bad as it had. They were so different now. Alien to each other. From twins to strangers.

God. His best friend was dead and his brother might as well be for all the contact they had with each other. No wonder Wise felt like he was barely keeping it together. He must've really pissed someone off in another life to keep getting smashed apart like this.

Wise blinked away the memories as best he could as he tried to force his mind back to the streets, to the now, but that much guilt knew how to hang around. It had its hooks deep into his very soul.

Shit. He needed some sleep. Get his thoughts back in order. Bury the past in the back of his mind as best he could. He had Hassleman to concentrate on. People who needed him.

At least there was a parking spot outside his house for once. Wise reversed the Mondeo into it, but he didn't turn the engine off. He stared at the four-bedroom terrace house, with its red door that he'd once happily painted, and tried to find the courage to go inside.

It was hard enough pretending to the people he worked with that everything was alright but it was all but impossible to fool the people who loved him.

Jean could see it and she wanted to help, but how? All he saw were his failings reflected in her eyes.

And then there were his kids, Ed and Claire. Nine and seven. Little Mister Sensible and Little Miss Chaos. The best parts of him and Jean all mixed into something new. Hopefully something better.

The love he felt for them was a burning light against all the darkness, the thing that held him together. Two wonderful little people that he'd do anything for. God, it hurt to see their love for him when he was crying inside.

Wise turned off the engine. Gathering his stuff, he got out of the car, locked it and headed into the house. Everything was so quiet that he felt like an unwelcome intruder, invading his family's tranquility. Even his key in the door lock turning sounded loud enough to wake the street.

Wise had to fight the urge to just turn around, get back in his car, and drive away. But he knew running wouldn't get him anywhere. It'd only make things worse. He'd run that night, from Tom, from they'd done, and he knew only too well the price he'd had to pay for that mistake. A price he was still paying.

Wise opened the door and stepped into the darkness. There was a glow upstairs, from the bathroom light left on and the door half-open, just in case one of the kids woke up and needed the loo.

He checked the time. 3:45. He'd have to leave by 7:45 to get to Kennington in time for the DMM. Factoring in time to shit, shower and shave, he had, maybe, three and a half hours to get some sleep.

Taking his shoes off, he trudged up the stairs. The spare room was to the left, the kids' room was straight ahead and then, after the bathroom, was his and Jean's room.

He stood on the landing, imagining them all asleep, hoping that they were all having happy dreams. He needed to find his way back to them somehow once he'd put all his ghosts to rest.

Wise turned left and headed to the spare room.

Alone.

THE DI SIMON WISE SERIES

Out Now:

Dead Man Running

Rich Men, Dead Men

The Killing Game

Coming soon:

Talking of the Dead (January 2024)

Printed in Great Britain
by Amazon

42040138R00069